PRAISE FOR SABRINA

"This is not only the retelling of the classic we all want, but is also the reforming of the idea behind who family is and where lies the good in one's life. A story of fulfilling purpose, finding courage, and freeing both minds and curses, *Blood Coven* is a walk through the darker side of those classic fairytale woods."

— GILLIAN DOWELL, AUTHOR OF
HELLO, DOVE

"Sabrina Voerman is a master wordsmith, weaving worlds and crafting characters excellently through powerful, elegant prose." -Brooklynn Dean, author of The Anti-Gospels Series

— BROOKLYNN DEAN, AUTHOR OF *THE ANTI-GOSPELS SERIES*

"Voerman makes of her prose a wilderness: sentences that ensnare like sharp branches, lush blooming words, an orchestra of wild nocturnal music that can beckon or bludgeon depending on her whims. This is a writer with a bright future, and *Blood Coven* presents one of the most sympathetic illustrations of lycanthropy that I've had the pleasure of reading in years."

— JEREMY MEGARGEE, AUTHOR OF *HEARTS OF MONSTERS*

BLOOD COVEN

BLOOD COVEN

THE BLOOD BOUND SERIES
BOOK 1

SABRINA VOERMAN

BLOOD COVEN: THE BLOOD BOUND SERIES, BOOK ONE
BY SABRINA VOERMAN
PUBLISHED BY QUILL & CROW PUBLISHING HOUSE

This book is a work of fiction. All incidents, dialogue, and characters are either products of the author's imagination or used in a fictitious manner. Any resemblance to actual persons, living or dead, or actual events is purely coincidental.

Copyright © 2023 by Sabrina Voerman

All rights reserved. Published in the United States by Quill & Crow Publishing House, Ohio. No portion of this book may be reproduced in any form without permission from the publisher, except as permitted by U.S. copyright law.

Cover Design by Fay Lane

Interior by Cassandra L. Thompson

Printed in the United States of America

ISBN (ebook) 978-1-958228-26-5

ISBN (print) 978-1-958228-30-2

Library of Congress Control Number: 2023912559

Publisher's Website: www.quillandcrowpublishinghouse.com

For my mother.
Thanks for telling everyone my book was published before it was,
so that I actually had to do it.

In the Mørke forest
    A Man does dwell
    Big eyes to seek you out

In the Mørke forest
    A Beast does prowl
    Big paws to match its snout

In the Mørke forest
    The Wolf does lurk
    Sharp teeth to make you shout

Obey all, young girl
    Or the Wolf Man of Mørke
    Will take you away, no doubt

— OLD SILVANIA LEGEND

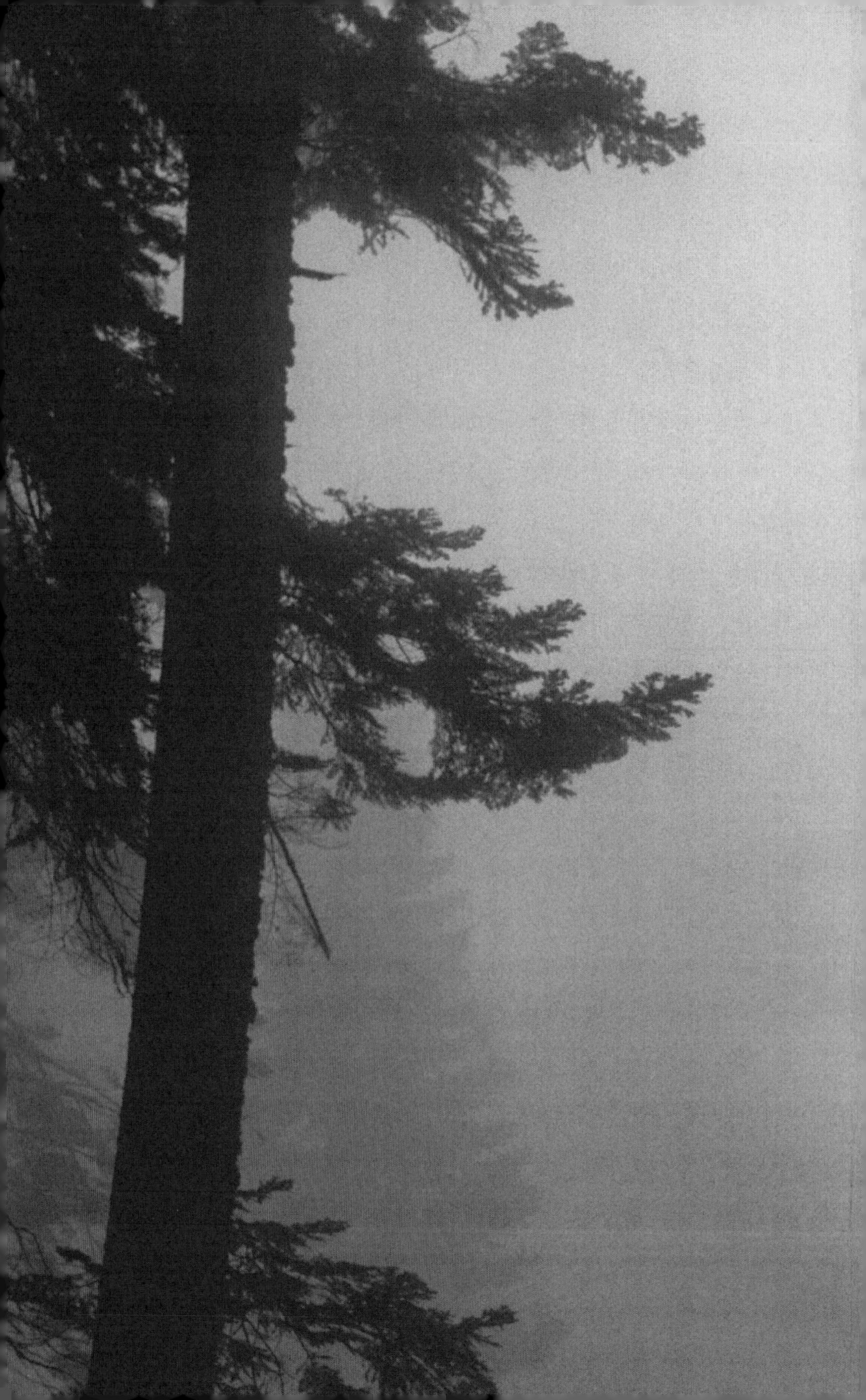

PROLOGUE

THE YEAR OF THE MOON

The eyes of the Mørke Forest bore into the man as he traversed the unkept pathway from town to his mother's home. It was as though the trees stretched their slender bodies to loom over him like curious spectators. Victor kept his eyes on the path; he did not trust the woods, for all manner of creatures dwelled within.

The steps to her house groaned and creaked as he climbed them. Though the house was newer than any in town, it had never been well-maintained. Its builder, his grandfather Adam, succumbed to madness before Victor was born. He did what he could to keep the roof patched and the walls from caving in.

"Mother?" he called into the shadows. The moon shone dimly above, offering only faint light through the windows. No candles were lit; there was no sign of life.

He heard the shuffle of shoes on the warped floorboards and the clunk of wood being moved. He opened the door and followed the sound to find his mother kneeling with her hands beneath the floor. Beside her was the floorboard she had removed. She lifted out a small locked box and offered it to him.

When he tried to take it, she refused to let go. Instead, she offered him a warning: "The cost of this curse. Do you know what it is?"

"Yes," Victor replied. "A daughter."

His mother scowled. Her face, barely visible in the faint glow from the filthy window, was withered, her lips curling and shrinking with age. Her brown eyes narrowed, appearing nearly black in the shadows. "Not just any daughter."

"This family was once in its prime. Your mother and father ran this town until that vampire-whore came and took everything, cursing us again, then fleeing back to Osleka..." he trailed off. "One small sacrifice, and the Wolf will do my bidding. He'll slaughter Fischer and his entire family. In one single night, this town will again be ours."

His mother smiled and released the box.

Victor grinned. Contained inside was a scroll bearing the incantation that allowed one to control the Wolf. One simple sacrifice and a bloodline would be massacred, allowing them to rise again.

"Kill the mayor's family and bring back the glory to our family name, my son." She placed her wrinkled, ring-clad hand on Victor's cheek. Then she stepped back and handed him the key.

Her motherly kindness warmed him as he opened the box and studied the dust-covered scroll inside. It was nearly four hundred years old, yet it remained in impeccable condition. Witchcraft might have been forbidden, but it had preserved the scroll so it could be used forever. Their family would have it until time stopped. Over the last four centuries, it had fallen into the hands of others, but it always found its way back. His ancestors never knew how it happened.

Unrolling the parchment, Victor read aloud: *"'Hatred consumes; feed this craving once and for all, end the reasoning for my enmity. End the blood that drips from the family, end their reign. I sacrifice my living, breathing daughter; yours to take as you will. Take that which I love to end that which I hate.'"*

"Do what I could not," his mother said. For she had a son instead of a daughter, and the curse could not be enacted with the sacrifice of a male child. But Victor had been granted a daughter—a seventeen-year-old daughter named Rose.

Azalea

Juniper

Matthias — Rima

Elise

PART I
The Girl

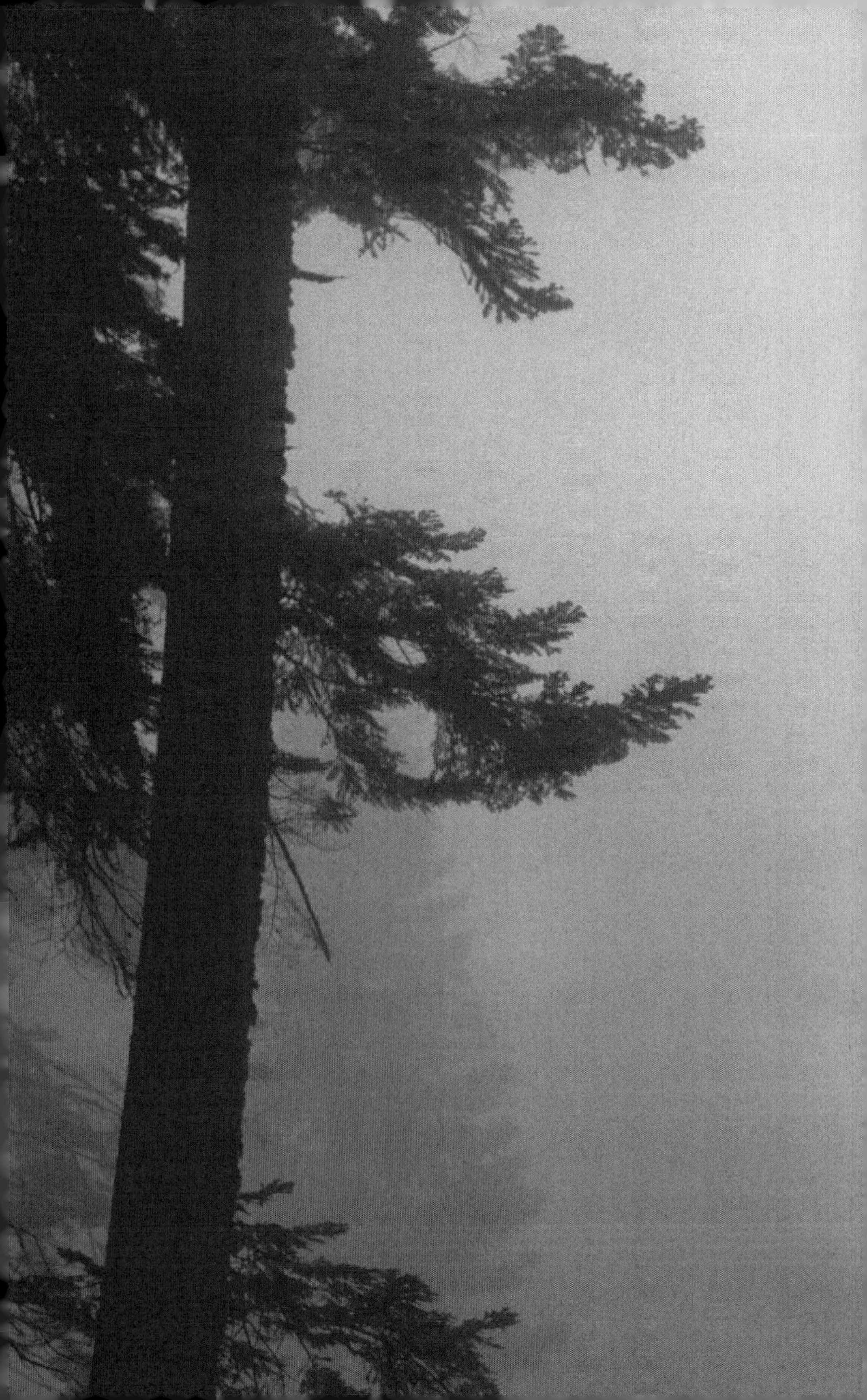

1

OCLEAU

THE YEAR OF THE CURSE (400 YEARS BEFORE THE YEAR OF THE MOON)

MATTHIAS

He crawled along the edges of the wilderness, fingers digging into the frozen dirt. His nails broke off along the way, leaving them jagged claws. His groans of agony echoed in the silence. No one was around to hear him, for he was miles away from any town. Though the sun appeared over the horizon, the moon still lingered in the lilac sky, taunting as it smiled down at him. Bright amber filled the treelines, making the condensation glitter like jewels.

The sensory onslaught caused him to squeeze his eyes shut in a desperate attempt to control the pounding in his temples. He curled into a ball, clutching his cold, naked body as the transition between wolf and man completed. Matthias whimpered, the childlike sound emerging involuntarily from his throat. He lay there for what felt like hours, thinking he would surely die of cold if the shock from the last twelve hours didn't kill him first. And yet, the morning sun rose and thawed the frost surrounding him, giving him the energy he needed to rise on shaking legs.

It was mid-afternoon when he finally arrived at the property he grew up on. It brought not a feeling of welcome but one of childhood horror. His rigid body slowed as he forced himself closer to the house that had never felt like home. Scant sunlight broke through the canopy, shining on a basket of linens on the porch. Desperate for heat and something to cover his fully exposed skin, he pulled an off-white sheet from the basket and pulled it around his shoulders. It offered him little warmth, and his mother's scent lingered on the fabric.

He could see the reddish glow of firelight through the thick, animal-skin windows, but he sensed no immediate movement inside. From the second-story roof, the chimney puffed out smoke in great plumes. Dread filled him as he mounted the steps. In moments, his presence in Ocleau would become known to the person he despised most in this world. There was still time to leave, to turn around and knock on someone else's door. But no one in town would open their doors to him, not if they knew who he was. Even if they did not recognize him, they certainly wouldn't welcome him stark naked and covered in dirt and blood.

Nearly to the door, his energy diminished, and he stumbled. The wooden steps cut into his bare shins, bruising them as he crawled, unable to get back on his feet. Despite the cold, a sheen of sweat coated his neck and back. The thump of his body falling should have caused alarm within the home. He slammed his fists into the door, feeling the peeling wood against his skin as his hands slid down its length. If no one answered, he had nowhere else to go.

When it finally opened and a pair of women's shoes appeared in sight, he tasted regret like bitter bile on his tongue.

"I always knew you'd come crawling back to me, Matthias," Azalea Luca said smugly.

"Spare me your lectures," he spat back at her, but his voice failed to maintain his hatred. Instead, it sounded strained. The words scraped his throat as though they fought to come up.

Her appearance surprised him as he looked up at her from his spot on the ground. She had aged in the years since he left, but not poorly. Deep-set creases engraved her skin yet, there was still beauty in the contours of her face. Both of them had the same deep-set brown eyes and brown hair that had run in the family for generations; hers had grayed. Yet, despite the smugness in her voice, a crease had formed between her brows, betraying her worry.

After all, he was still her son.

"Come in," she said, helping him inside. "I believe I have some of your old clothes lying about."

After finding him something to wear, she disappeared into the kitchen to make something to warm him. Matthias let the sheet fall to the ground and dressed, pain and stiffness slowing his movements. It felt as though he'd been ripped in half; he was almost certain his body had been. The clothes were snug, pinching into his skin. He had been so young when he left town, barely a man. Fully dressed, Matthias knelt on the warped wooden floor before the fire, his arms extended so he could thaw his fingers in the warmth of the flames.

"Here," she said, thrusting a piping hot mug of tea into his hands.

He nodded his thanks before sipping at the steaming liquid. It was so bitter that he nearly spit it out but forced himself to swallow it. His insides warmed, and he knew he would recover shortly. But recovery meant nothing if he had to face what he had suffered again. Fear crept back as he recalled his body twisting into a monstrous beast. He could not go through it again.

"Tell me everything," his mother demanded, kneeling beside him and placing her wrinkled hands on his arm.

Matthias shifted, shrugging her hand away and putting distance between them. He had no desire to be touched, especially by her. But he needed her if he wanted to be free from whatever curse had been forced upon him. His voice still raked through his throat, and pain sliced through his tongue. He suspected it was the transformation that made speaking so painful.

"You told me...as a child to stay...out of the Mørke Forest during the full moon. Why?" The words caught as he struggled to free them.

Azalea exhaled sharply, rising to tend to the fire. As she stared into the flames with her back turned to Matthias, he could see the tension in her shoulders. It was apparent from her concern and how she avoided his gaze that this was not how she expected him to return. She finally turned and looked at him, the contempt gone from her gaze. Fear replaced it, narrowing her eyes and making the corners of her lips pull downward. Anything that his foul creature of a mother feared would terrify anyone else ten-fold. "Tell me what happened, Matthias."

If he wanted to be cured, he had to obey. Whatever she demanded of him, he had to do it. He began to speak, though it felt like his throat was closing. He paused every few words. "Three days ago, I was hunting, tracking a deer deep in the forest. When I finally caught up to her, I realized I was not the only one hunting her. There was a wolf pack, four or five of them. Two struck the doe, and one...he went for me. They left me for dead, seeing me as a rival hunter and took out the competition.

"But I did not die nor succumb to my wounds. That night...something happened to me, Azalea." He knew using her name would upset her, but he refused to call her Mother; mothers didn't do to their children what Azalea had done to him. "I became one of them," he continued. "I could feel them all around me, smell exactly where they had been. It became necessary to follow, to find them. I fought the instinct, though, and I suppose in my moment of sanity—or delirium —I wound up a few miles from here as the sun rose."

By the time he finished, his frustration at his difficulty speaking was at capacity. It felt like he had swallowed hot rocks.

"And now you have returned to me. For what?"

"Get it out of me."

"Very well," she said, unspoken words dangling at the end of her agreement.

"What is your price?" He looked up and met her steely gaze. Deep down, Matthias knew that what she wanted most in this world was the one thing he could not give her. Before the words came out of her mouth, he could hear them rattling around in her head and saw the thoughts forming in her eyes. In the past, Azalea had done everything in her power to ensure her son never left and, in doing so, forced him away. Now she held the power to ask anything she wanted, and he knew what it was.

"You must never leave."

2

SILVANIA

THE YEAR OF THE MOON

RED

Her father shouted, the sound reverberating through the house. Red kept silent. She waited patiently in her warm crimson cloak with her wavy brown hair pulled back in a neat bun. Her daily chores always ended with a trip to her grandmother's before sunset, but today, she was forced to wait while her father yelled at her mother. She hummed to drown it out, her rumbling stomach soon competing with her tune. She tried not to think of her hunger as she peered out the front window of the house. Their home sat at the end of town, with vast acreage behind them, most of it unkempt. They could not afford the upkeep.

The skies were lined with streaks of pinks and blues stretching as far as she could see; Red knew if she didn't hurry, she would walk home from her grandmother's in the dark. The hair on the back of her neck raised as she thought about what lurked in those woods. The feeling that the forest breathed down her neck never went away. Red closed her eyes to calm herself, but when she opened them, her heart lurched. Standing at the end of the path was a woman watching her through the window. Red felt naked, exposed, as the ghost-like girl studied her as if she could hear her every thought. She leaned in and squinted to get a better look, realizing it was Alina.

Red's breath caught in her chest. The memory of last week's meeting came flooding back to her. She almost tasted the stale air of the meeting hall.

Mayor Fischer spoke loudly at the forefront while the town's youth shifted nervously in their seats. The wood benches, constructed from the deciduous trees of Mørke Forest, were nearly filled.

"Obeying your parents will bring you prosperity," Mayor Fischer continued. It was the same speech he gave each week to the village youth. Every child who dwelled in their family home was forced to attend, lest they bring dishonor and punishment to their families.

Red sat in the middle, where she was surrounded by the others and yet perfectly invisible. So long as she sat with her back straight and her head high, no one questioned her attentiveness. Mayor Fischer's voice filled the hall with a superiority that reminded her of her father's.

Underneath the safety of her bonnet, she could spare glances at the others. As she did every week, she sought out one person in particular. Her white-blonde hair was easy to spot. The moment Red found Alina Nastaca, a woman beside her turned as though she knew Red was looking. She averted her gaze and sharply inhaled.

"Rose, are you alright?" a boy's voice startled Red.

She looked to her right and saw Sebastian, Mayor Fischer's son, with concern etched onto his boyish features.

Red nodded and looked away.

Everyone around her began to stand—it was time for the building portion of the day. To show the others what she could offer to the community. All Red had was the bread her mother had helped her bake and a jar of freshly churned butter. Last week the bread had not risen, and the mayor expressed his disappointment with a few words about her impending failure to satisfy her future husband.

Red had no desire ever to satisfy a husband. The very thought made her stomach roil.

Red clutched her basket with sweaty hands as everyone began to mingle and show off their new skill, be it embroidery, sewing, or blacksmithing. Surely no one will dare try my baking again, she thought.

She jumped when a hand touched her shoulder.

"Rose, you mustn't be frightened so easily. Certainly not by me," Sebastian said, removing his hand. He was just one year younger than Red but never grew out of his childish looks. His round cheeks always looked flushed, as though he'd been running in the cold, paired with a slightly crooked nose.

"I'm not afraid of you," she replied, finding her voice. It was true; she wasn't afraid of Sebastian. She was afraid of what could happen should a boy find her pretty enough to seek her affections.

Behind Sebastian, Alina was approached by the mayor. He gestured to her hair and said something Red couldn't hear. Alina merely looked down at her loose locks and shrugged. Mayor Fischer shook his head and gripped her shoulder.

Red felt the blood in her veins ripple with disdain. Sebastian was speaking to her, but she heard nothing.

"Excuse me," she said.

Leaving Sebastian behind, she hurried through the crowd towards Alina and the mayor. When she was close enough, she made brief eye contact. For a moment, every word disappeared from her thoughts. "Mayor Fischer, you must try what I've baked," she finally managed.

Alina, who had previously looked bemused, let the corner of her lip creep upward. Her eyes lit up with understanding and appreciation.

The mayor sighed, released Alina, and turned his attention to Red. "Rose, I was speaking with Alina."

"Your words about my inability to satisfy my future husband perturbed me." The words coated Red's tongue with disgust. "Please, I must know if this will suffice." She thrust out the basket and pulled back the cloth, revealing a perfectly risen loaf with marks etched in the crust just as Mama had shown her.

As the mayor reached in, Alina caught Red's eyes and mouthed, "Thank you."

Her heart fluttered even as Alina left the hall, fleeing before the mayor could chastise her any further. Red didn't listen to the feedback the mayor had to offer. Her ears were crimson, and she heard her blood throbbing in her head. She nodded along and mumbled, "Yes, sir," when she thought it appropriate.

"Papa!" Celeste, the mayor's daughter, was in tears. She tugged at his hand, pulling his attention away from Red.

Red slipped out of the hall while she could, not wanting to be caught by any more of the Fischer family. Though they were kinder than her own family, they left her exhausted. The autumn sun was soft upon her skin, and Red leaned against the side of the building. She closed her eyes to calm herself down.

"Thank you, Red."

Red's eyes bolted open, and all the calmness she had mustered evaporated. It was Alina, the one who gave Rose the nickname Red for the crimson cloak she wore each day.

"You're welcome," Red replied, unable to shake the jitters from her voice.

"Let me offer this as a token of my gratitude," Alina said. She reached into the bag draped over her shoulder and pulled out a bundle of sticks wrapped in a strip of fabric.

Red took it from her. "What's this?"

"I tell the others it's a fire starter," Alina said. "But I'll let you in on a secret."

Red could hardly contain her nerves. They sparked like flames with every breath. A wind blew over the tops of the trees, rustling the leaves. The branches rattled, and half a dozen leaves were released, fluttering through the air as they fell to the ground.

"They're magic," she said. "Imbued with an ancient power."

"Alina..." Red trailed off. She dared not accuse Alina of witchcraft. *Mama warned me of the temptations of witchcraft—that I'll be drawn to it because of my blood,* she thought.

"They will burn for longer than regular wood," Alina explained. A sympathetic look crossed over her face. "And they ward off anyone who wishes you ill will, should you choose to burn it."

"I—"

"Place it in your hearth tonight," Alina whispered, "and your father will forget you're there."

The bell signaling midday struck. The metal clang echoed through the village, followed by a few dozen children and young adults running from the hall. Joyous shouts in anticipation for a few hours of play overtook the bell.

Red looked down at the generosity Alina gifted her. *I cannot accept this,* she thought. With a heart torn in two pieces, she thrust the bundle back at Alina and turned on her heel...

Tears had welled up in her eyes as she hurried home. The regret of not accepting a gift from the woman who made her body stir with desire followed her the entire way. It struck her again, now, as she looked at Alina out the window.

"Get up, Rose. You're going to be late." Her mother's voice snapped her out of her daze. She thrust a wicker basket of food at her. "You know how your grandmother feels about tardiness."

Red hurried out the door. Thankfully, Alina was no longer there. She couldn't afford any distractions, especially with the way Alina made her heart race.

The sun dipped below the naked treeline. Red knew it would be impossible to arrive on time. The wicker basket, full of Mama's fresh baked loaves, weighed down the crook of her elbow, chafing the skin through her blouse. To walk in the woods after dark was a danger Red didn't like to risk. Her mother had warned her to stay on the path and never wander into the Mørke Forest.

Red walked quickly, though her feet ached. Her stomach twisted, empty from having another meal taken from her by her father. She reluctantly slowed, knowing she could not keep up such a brisk pace without sustenance. *I should have taken Alina's gift,* she thought. She studied the trees surrounding her, relieved she neared her destination.

The decrepit old house would soon appear around the corner—or perhaps the next. The closer she got to her grandmother's, all the trees looked the same. The bitter autumn air sank deep into her lungs, creeping up her sleeves and biting her flesh. Red resumed her hurried pace, terrified of what she might find in the woods after dark. Her breath fogged in front of her. Though her grandmother was cold-hearted and cruel, her hearth would be warm. That alone was enough for Red to accept whatever brutality she would face when she arrived.

A giggle in the depths of the forest startled Red, causing her skid to a stop, dirt flying around her brown boots. With wide eyes and a hammering heart, she scoured the shadows for the source. In the distance, she saw the flickering light of distant fire. Fire meant warmth. She took a few steps closer to the forest but paused when she reached the edge of the path. Her body refused to break the rule she had always followed. *"Never stray from the path."* Her mother's words rattled inside her skull.

Red had abided by this rule since she was a child, obeying her order never to leave the town boundary except to go to her grandmother's. She dared not stray from the path, even as the forest began to reclaim it.

"Who's there?" Red shouted, shocking herself with the outburst. She immediately wished she had remained silent. *I should have gone straight to Grandmother's like I was supposed to.* Danger lived in those forests, and drawing attention to herself was a mistake she couldn't afford. Young women did not belong in the woods after dark.

There was no breeze, but the trees whispered in the voices of girls. A form began to take shape, approaching Red. The apparition encroached, and she began to quiver.

"Ghosts aren't real," she whispered to herself, but it did little to ease her worry. Humans could be so much worse.

But as the form paused an arm's length away from Red, she saw it was not a ghost. The woman who stood before her was short in stature and strikingly beautiful. As she studied her wraith-like hair and the nightgown that clung to her lithe frame, Red recognized Alina. Had she been outside Red's home earlier to lure her here?

"Alina." Red breathed out the name in a whisper. "What are you doing out here?"

Alina laughed, a burst that ripped through the air, disturbing the silence of the forest.

When she did not receive an answer, Red stumbled and stammered. "There are dark and dangerous things in these woods, Alina. You should not be out here."

"We are the dark and dangerous things in these woods, Red." When she smiled, it reached her hazel eyes. "Why don't you join us?"

"Us?" Red asked, searching behind her. In the distance, she saw the fire flickering, but when she focused, she swore she saw a pair of glowing eyes. She blinked in a desperate attempt to rid herself of the illusion, but the eyes lingered when she opened hers again.

Alina kept a serene smile on her face in reply.

Maybe Alina wasn't trying to trick her, Red thought, as the other kids did. No one uttered Red's family name without distaste on the tongue. Unwelcome at home and unwelcome in town, she never had friends, forced instead to watch other children playing in the distance. With this offer before her, she grappled with the idea, savoring the thought.

The Mørke Forest is where evil things dwell, Red thought ruefully. *Mama always said the worst crime is witchcraft.*

"I—I should not. I could not," she stammered at last. "I must get to my grandmother's before dark."

"Very well, but know that the offer stands, Red. We could use someone like you in our group." Alina's tone hinted at the depth of her secrets. "It's things that come out at night that are so much more exciting."

The promise of friendship beckoned to Red. Unable to continue to look into Alina's enticing eyes, Red cast hers to the ground. "I am sorry," she mumbled. "I cannot."

As she shuffled away, gathering her skirt and continuing to her grandmother's, Red felt a twinge of sadness at leaving behind her first chance at friendship. She felt eyes on her as she continued down the path without looking back. She knew if she did, she would be lured into the warm welcome of other girls. Girls who wanted to include her in whatever they were up to. Her mother's warnings trickled in.

Only two things lurked in the woods—wolves and witches.

Arriving at her grandmother's at last, Red carefully knocked on the door. The house had always looked like it would collapse at any moment. From what she knew, her great-grandfather had left the town when he started to lose his mind; he escaped to the woods, where he built their ramshackle home.

Red strained to hear the old woman call her in. When she heard her grandmother's voice, she knew she was in trouble. Her hands shook as she entered. The woman shuffled out from the back, where the single bedroom was.

"I've brought you Mama's bak—" A sharp backhand to the cheek cut Red off, her grandmother's rings slicing into her skin. She reached up to clutch her bleeding cheek. Her grandmother yanked the wicker basket from her arm, chafing her tender forearms through her sleeves.

"You're an hour late," she snapped. "What were you doing? Did you stray from the path?"

The old woman grabbed a fistful of Red's hair, bringing it to her nose and inhaling. Searching for the smell of earth and bonfire smoke.

Her grandmother shuffled away, placing the basket on the table. She did not immediately take out the bread as usual and instead disappeared. When she returned, she brought out a stick. Red whimpered, tears burning the fresh cut on her cheek. The gentle sting was nothing compared to what was coming.

"Please, I did not stray!" Red cried. "I promise!"

A slap to her other cheek made Red turn away. She clutched the swollen flesh and looked up pleadingly at her grandmother.

"You speak out of turn," the old woman growled, then dropped the stick. It clattered loudly on the ground. "Kneel."

Red bit her lip to hold back the sobs as she shuffled towards the stick, placing her knees atop it. The warped and knotted wood dug into her knees. No matter how she shifted her body, it dug into a sensitive part of the joint and made her cry out. The worn-down cartilage in her knees sparked with pain, yesterday's bruises sending agony shooting through her like a bolt of lightning.

Her grandmother sat at the table and smiled as she watched her granddaughter's torment. She pulled out the bread and other freshly baked goods, the scent wafting through the house. Red's stomach growled. The crunch of crust and crumbs dropping to the floor were the only sounds beyond the occasional crackle of the fire and Red's quiet sobs.

"Disobedience is as wicked and foul as witchcraft," her grandmother snarled as she wiped butter grease from her face with the hem of her shawl. A feral grin curled at the corners of her thin, concave lips. "Do you know what happens to disobedient girls? The Wolf will come and snatch them away, never to be seen again."

Red would have scowled if she wasn't gritting her teeth to hold back her tears. Stories from her childhood bubbled up to the forefront of her mind: tales of a Wolf called upon to decimate an entire bloodline through a sacrifice. No one knew if it was true. Some believed the Wolf would eat the young women who strayed from the path their parents put them on.

It's just a bedtime story, Red thought. But when she looked up at her grandmother smiling through her gluttony, she began to doubt herself.

"You're going to regret being such a wretched child. Don't you worry. Justice is coming for you."

Red shifted, and a small knot caused a spark of pain to rip through her. Hot tears continued to slip down the torn flesh of her cheeks. Thoughts of the Wolf filled her head again at her grandmother's words. She did not know for how long she knelt. All she knew was that the sun was long gone by the time she was free to go.

As she limped miserably through the woods, she was struck by a thought: compared to the horrors she faced from her own flesh and blood, witchcraft and the things that stirred in the night no longer seemed so frightening.

3

OCLEAU

THE YEAR OF THE CURSE

MATTHIAS

A tense silence filled the Luca household; only the crackling fire made any noise. Matthias carefully considered the decision before him, wondering if his life would be worth living if he had to remain in Ocleau.

Years ago, he vowed never to return, no matter how desperate he became. But the curse now running through his veins was more dire than any consequence he had ever faced. Balancing his limited options quickly in his head, he found few reasons to stay, but the weight of being freed from this curse was certainly worth considering.

Then he thought of *her* and what Azalea did to her. His hands curled into fists until his knuckles turned white.

Matthias had been young but not entirely blinded by love. He was mature enough to know that *she* was the only person he wanted in this world, so he had waited for her all those months. Full of hope for their future, he had gone down to the river where they always met, knowing they would soon leave Ocleau together. The rocks along the shore shifted under his feet, threatening to twist an ankle if he wasn't careful. He scanned the riverbed in search of her. His chest expanded with a wretched terror when he eventually found a womanly frame half-submerged in the water. The rapids pulled at her dress and legs, but enough of her body rested ashore that she wasn't swept away. As if someone placed her there so he would see.

He raced toward her, his ankle inevitably twisting on a rock that gave out beneath him. The pain didn't register until later. Matthias collapsed beside his lover's body; her skin was slick with river slime, her striking features lost beneath the bloat.

While he could never find evidence that his mother committed the crime, he left everything behind all the same. The townsfolk of Ocleau believed him guilty so he was forced to leave, unable to prove his mother was the reason *she* was dead. His mother drove him away when she killed the woman he loved, but it was the townsfolk who forced him to stay gone. He hoped, after all these years, they'd have forgotten the murder and his face.

Matthias banished the memories, but his chest tightened, protecting his heart. He couldn't bear the thought of living out the remainder of his life at a murderer's beck and call.

As though she read his mind, she said, "The wolves that attacked you are most likely a pack. There is a good chance they will return for you when the full moon rises. I can see that you believe this might not be as bad as you thought; a pack of people just like you." She stared at him. "Only they are not like you, Matthias. You are an honest, righteous man. The people who choose the cursed life—"

"People like you?" he asked, his tone bitter. "People who choose to do evil, who do witchcraft and kill innocents?"

Azalea narrowed her brown eyes. "I have never killed an innocent person."

"I beg to differ," Matthias growled as he stood up, towering over his mother.

She continued, unfazed. "There have been werewolf trials throughout the continent. Men and women have been found naked and covered in blood after the nights of the full moon, surrounded by slaughtered livestock and even their own family members. Very few can control their impulses under the moon curse—the scent of familiarity brings them home, where they wake to their wives and children ripped apart by their own hands."

Matthias stared his mother down. "Perhaps in a month's time, I will have your blood on my hands. Trust me. I will not feel an ounce of guilt."

Before she could retort, the door hinges' groan filled the house, silencing them both. Matthias looked up to see the only person who could convince him to stay. His little sister entered the house gracefully, her bare feet padding along the floor.

It had been ten years since he last saw her, and she had evolved from a skinny eleven-year-old into a beautiful young woman. Only her green eyes remained unchanged. Her gaze met her brother's, and her face erupted into a grin. She dropped her basket of autumn mushrooms and berries, and rushed to throw her arms around his neck and shoulders.

Matthias hugged her back; she smelled of the damp forests and hints of lavender. Her waist-length brown hair was a mess from being out in the woods.

Finally, she released him, continuing to stare as she beamed. "Brother..."

"Juniper, I am so glad to see you," he said. His only regret had been leaving her behind, but he could never have offered her the shelter and safety that Azalea could. Matthias had always known his sister would follow their mother's path into witchcraft. But while Azalea was cruel, Juniper possessed something she didn't: compassion.

"Why have you returned?" she asked him. "You look and sound dreadful. Has something happened?"

Matthias placed a hand on her shoulder. "I have not come on good terms."

"But he is staying," Azalea added. "Unless, of course, he chooses death."

"What is she talking about?" Juniper stared at Matthias, then glanced at her mother when she didn't get an answer. "Mama, what are you saying? He finally returns home, and already you force him out?"

Azalea raised a conspicuous eyebrow but said nothing. Her expression made it clear that she expected him to fill his sister in, to admit that he had failed at keeping himself safe and had come crawling back for help. But Matthias wasn't going to let Azalea control him. He turned his attention back to Juniper. If he speculated correctly, she too would be a successful witch like their mother by now, and perhaps she could help him without the ultimatum.

I hope after all these years, Azalea hasn't corrupted Juniper.

He looked into the green eyes that didn't belong in their family and sighed. "I was attacked by a pack of wolves, and now I fear my fate is to be one of them."

"The moon curse," Juniper gasped, expression softening with pity and sorrow.

Matthias nodded.

"Mama, you must get it out of him," Juniper demanded, turning towards their mother. "I care not for your differences; he is your son. He is my brother. What is your cost? What are you asking of him?"

"A life for a life," Azalea said simply, clasping her hands before her. "I save his life. He remains with us in Ocleau—to protect us."

"We do not need protection," Juniper argued. "We can handle the trespassers."

"Have you had trouble?" Matthias asked, directing the question to his mother. Like most towns, Ocleau forbade witchcraft, and, like most towns, it chose to overlook the town witch because she was useful. So far, Ocleau had not burned, hanged, or crushed a single witch. Yet.

"Rocks thrown at the house, threats, someone tried to start a fire..." Juniper admitted. "It is nothing we cannot handle ourselves." But her tone betrayed her fear. She turned her attention to Azalea. "Mama, do not make him agree to your terms."

"Then say goodbye to your beloved brother again, child," Azalea sneered. "For when he wakes with the blood of others on his hands in a month's time, he will be put on trial and killed for what he has become."

"Azalea, that is enough." Matthias croaked, exhausted. "Only when you prove you can rid me of this curse will I consider your conditions."

Azalea turned her back to her children and marched to a book-covered table, where candles had dripped wax pools on the worn, weathered surface. She shuffled through the artifacts, some old enough to crumble if held too tightly. Within seconds, she dug out a book and carried it back to the fire.

She flipped through the pages, her eyes darting back and forth until she found what she sought. She twisted the book, so Juniper and Matthias could read. It felt wrong to gaze upon the forbidden words, but Matthias was desperate.

Juniper nodded carefully. "Yes, displacement. Of course. I was thinking the very same."

"Displacement? What does that mean?" Matthias asked, looking between his mother and his sister.

"It means we must take the curse from you and put it into someone else. The curse cannot simply be removed. It must go somewhere, or rather, into another body," Juniper explained.

"So, someone else must suffer my fate?" Matthias asked weakly, his stomach sinking at the thought.

"Moreso, they must be willing," Azalea added.

4

SILVANIA

THE YEAR OF THE MOON

RED

Her knees cried with every step she took toward home, making her feel as old as her grandmother. Her posture slanted from the throbbing in her lower back. Tears continued to sting the cuts on her cheek. The unrelenting forest path took advantage of her trembling state, tripping her twice. The second time, she fell on all fours. As she crouched, she wondered if she would even be able to get up. With hands bleeding from the rocks that dug into her flesh, she crawled forward another few meters before two pairs of bare feet appeared. They almost seemed to glow, pale in the moonlight that filled the sky.

Red glanced up at the hand extended to her. With fear in her stomach, not knowing what accepting this hand would mean for her, Red grabbed hold of it. Standing before her were two strikingly beautiful brunettes, their smiles and oval-shaped faces nearly identical. She realized they were the Floarea sisters. Tatiana was the same age as Red, and Lilianna was younger by two years. Rumors passed through the town of their mischief, blaming them for all sorts of trouble, including stealing pies from window sills and releasing rats into local establishments.

But the smiles they wore now were not threatening; they were friendly and sympathetic. Lilianna had a twig in her hair as though she had been rolling in the dirt, her mess of locks giving her the appearance that she was more child than young woman. By contrast, Tatiana's features spoke of cunning wit paired with something almost matronly. Red knew Tatiana took over many roles in the Floarea home when their mother died. Her pale green eyes swam with understanding. Her extended hand was a gesture of...what? *No one ever helps me off my knees; people only put me there.*

Tatiana spoke first. "You best stay out with us, Red." She gestured to Red's hands, covered in dirt and blood. "You'll be much safer out here."

Lilianna chimed in. "Everyone knows what happens within the walls of your home. We've seen your bruises from a distance." She leaned in to study Red's cheeks. "Up close, they are much worse."

Shame spread throughout Red's body, and she cast her eyes to the ground, focusing on her tattered shoes.

Tatiana put two fingers underneath Red's chin, gently lifting her face so she looked them in the eyes again.

"I am already late," Red whispered sheepishly.

"Exactly." Lilianna grinned. "If you never return home, they cannot touch you."

Tatiana grabbed both of Red's ice-cold hands; hers were so warm, they almost burned. *How could they be so warm when they were out in the chill?*

Tatiana seemed to answer the thoughts on her mind. "We can help protect you. It's what we do."

"Protect me how?" Red asked, curiosity and terror rushing through her at the same time. She worried following them would lead to something far worse than abuse when she returned home.

"Come." Lilianna stood a few steps away, beckoning for Red and Tatiana to follow her. She walked back toward the glow of the fire that had been there when Red first passed by. Lilianna's long mousy hair reached her mid-back, partially tucked into the strap of her white dress. All the girls Red had seen so far wore white nightgowns. Such garments were far too intimate to wear outdoors, particularly in this cold. And yet it was Red, clad in her crimson cloak and thick winter skirt, who shivered in the cold.

Before she knew it, she was following Lilianna while Tatiana walked beside her, holding her shaking hand. Soon, two other girls came into view, looking like wraiths dancing around the fire. She recognized Alina, her arms waving above her head, observing everything around her. The other figure moved too wildly for Red to see. As if she knew what Red was thinking, she paused long enough to make eye contact. Red recoiled.

Everyone knew Sorin was a witch.

"Red," Sorin said with a gentle nod of her head. Her dress had slipped over one of her dark shoulders. She gracefully stepped around the roaring fire and stopped just before Red. A giant rat sat on her other shoulder, peering up from underneath the fabric of her nightgown. Sorin lifted her hand and touched Red's blushing cheek. "We've been expecting you."

"Y-you have?" Red asked, studying the illuminated faces of all four girls.

"You are very important to us, for you have a gift," Alina said, stepping closer to Red.

"I th-think you are mistaken," Red stammered, but deep down, she knew Alina was right. *It's in my blood,* she reminded herself as she looked at the tall, imposing witch standing before her. Her eyes darted to Sorin's rat.

"Put that creature away, Sorin. You're going to scare her!" Tatiana scolded.

Sorin grabbed the rat from her shoulder and held its plump body in both hands, tilting her head back and lifting it over her head. The rat reached for her, its little claws scraping her lips. She kissed it on the nose and placed it back on her shoulder, where it nestled into her black hair.

The rat's beady eyes stared into Red, the flames flickering.

"Lucien likes you," Sorin said, stroking the rat gently. "Are you scared, Red?"

These feelings; are they fear? Red wasn't sure. She was thrilled by the new stirrings inside her, yet she knew what happened to girls who lingered in the forest and dabbled in the forbidden Craft.

She looked around, avoiding Sorin's sharp stare. Alina's gaze was no less foreboding, yet Red felt safe around her. Tatiana and Lilianna still smiled with welcoming expressions and softness. They were the youngest of the group. Alina was almost nineteen, and Sorin was quite a bit older, her age unknown to Red. The only person who moved to Silvania in Red's lifetime was Sorin Nabita.

"I must go home," Red told them. "I wish to stay, I do…but I fear what will happen should I return home any later than I already am."

A solemn look crossed all their faces, but it was Alina who spoke. "You are always welcome here. We will never lay a hand on you."

"Unless," Sorin added with a grin, "you want us to."

Alina had something in her hands and stepped up to Red with careful, calculated movements. With a tender raise of her hand, she gently rubbed something on the cuts in Red's cheeks; her soft fingertips and the cool salve made the throbbing of the wounds ebb. Alina showed her decency no one else had ever done before. Their eyes met and held, unlike the other times Alina caught Red watching her, and they both looked away.

Does Alina watch me from a distance as I watch her? The thought terrified and thrilled her all at once, but terror won, and Red turned on her heel, her wounds tingling as they healed.

Red ran the rest of the way home, ignoring her body's lingering aches and pains.

The houses along the muddy path in town glowed with firelight and candles, lighting her way. She heard loud music and rowdy laughter roaring inside as she passed the tavern. She glanced at the newest building in town, the only establishment that brought people together. Long ago, Red's ancestors had burned down the previous brothel and the Madame who owned it. But all manner of wicked things stay in high demand, and it was not long before it was rebuilt from the ashes.

The lantern hanging at the front of Red's home shuddered in the wind. She froze at the front door. Dread filled her as she wiped her hands on the front of her skirt, clearing away the crusted blood and dirt that remained. She was not presentable, and she was late, but none of it really mattered. The result would be the same. Entering the house, she knew what she would face: another missed meal, perhaps a physical punishment, then off to bed.

It was just another day.

5

OCLEAU

THE YEAR OF THE CURSE

MATTHIAS

Waking in a bed too small for him, Matthias wrinkled his nose at the smell that settled in overnight. Musty bedding and the essence of something brewing downstairs greeted his senses, forcing him to rise. His childhood bedroom smelled stale, as though nothing had changed since he left. The very air seemed to be waiting for him to return and breathe it in again.

Everything sat where he remembered it when he stormed out of the house ten years ago at nineteen. The straw-filled bed still sat under a window so grime-covered he couldn't see through it. The far side of the bedroom was nestled into the a-frame of the roof, so when he stood straight up, he hit his head. A chest sat by the door where he knew he would find his clothes, as though his mother had always known he would return.

Clad in clean breaches that didn't fit him properly and a tunic with creases from being folded too long, Matthias went downstairs to see Azalea and Juniper. A familiar and almost homey feel slammed into him as he reached the landing where the stairs turned. He paused to observe Juniper kneeling before the fire, breaking dried flowers into the cauldron that hung over a low flame. Azalea was in the kitchen, barely visible behind the herbs and plants hanging from the ceiling. Something smelled delicious.

"Good morning," Juniper said without looking over her shoulder. Despite focusing intently on her task, she was in tune with everything around her.

She's done alright without me; she's a survivor. Still, he worried. So much that it made him consider staying. Witch burnings were happening more and more often in other towns. Azalea had even mentioned attacks on the house; their lives were in constant danger from aggravated townsfolk. He knew it was not a lie because Juniper supported it, and his sister was not a liar. No matter Azalea's influence, he believed she was still the girl who took in wounded animals and nursed them back to health. The girl who built wooden homes for birds and bats alike. Juniper loved all living things; she was innocent and just. He had to believe that if nothing else.

He descended the rest of the stairs to join them.

"Eat," Azalea commanded as she shoved a plate of fresh bread with a heap of melting butter his way. The metal plate dug into his ribs before he could grab it. Despite his irritation, he ate ravenously. Hunger was not easily ignored.

"Thank you for breakfast," Matthias said cautiously when he finished, his stomach not yet full but his craving satisfied. Giving Azalea thanks was his way of keeping her happy. *If she believes I'm giving her a second chance, maybe she'll reconsider her deal,* he thought. If she tried to keep him around by being kind instead of using her witchcraft to murder the woman he loved, he would never have left in the first place.

"Your speech is coming back," Azalea remarked. "Very good."

"Yes. I suppose it was just a sore throat."

She scoffed at him, a sharp cackle escaping her lips. "A sore throat? No, Matthias, that is a side effect of the moon curse. Animals do not speak, so you lose your speech the more you shift. Each month, you will descend further and further into becoming a beast, losing your humanity. Eventually, you will no longer be able to speak or walk upright."

"I struggle to see how that is possible," he argued, glancing at his sister for confirmation.

Juniper looked at him briefly, then bowed and returned to her tasks.

Azalea walked up to him, her tall frame allowing her to look him in the eye. Her foreboding presence made her seem taller. "Use your head, Matthias. Every time you make the shift, your bones crack and break—they can only handle so much. Your vocal cords will eventually be so shredded that the only sounds you will be able to make are grunts. Tell me, do you wish for that?"

He stared her down, but without Juniper saying she was lying, Matthias was forced to believe her words. "No."

Her eyes betrayed no emotion as she stared at him, the flesh around them wrinkled. Deep creases around her mouth from years of frowning stretched when she spoke. "Then today, you must begin your search. It will not be an easy task. The full moon is in twenty-five days, and it must be done by then."

"Twenty-six," he corrected.

"The full moon lasts three days, Matthias. You will shift into a wolf for three nights and days, and each time will be more dangerous than the last. You'll have tasted blood the first time, and you will crave it," she explained.

He realized she was right: he had been attacked one night, then shifted the next. The days that went by blurred together from beginning to end. From the attack to the shift, to crawling back to his mother's doorstep, he had only a vague concept of time and a crisp awareness of danger and vulnerability.

He was still skeptical. "If others can live with this curse, why can't

I? If I were chained every full moon, I would not be a threat to anyone."

"Chains would only hold you until the authorities found you. Your howls would not go unheard, and your disgruntled state for days after every full moon would not go unnoticed."

"I'm sure others have succeeded—"

"It would take three months at best before they discovered you, and that is if you did not lose your mind by then."

"There has to be a way."

"You cannot take away a wolf's basic needs."

Juniper appeared before Matthias with a steaming mug, startling him. She watched him as he sipped at it, her forest-green eyes meeting his brown ones. "She speaks the truth, brother. While we have not encountered a werewolf here, I have traveled to nearby towns and witnessed the trials held for the afflicted. It's horrific to witness; after torture, it usually ends with burning or beheading. I do not wish to see you torn apart for something you cannot control. I only just got you back. I cannot lose you again."

Matthias wondered if Azalea told Juniper to say those words, their guilt-provoking effect making him ache to stay. To protect his sister at all costs, from the town...from their mother. No, Matthias thought. Juniper's choice has been made. She is a witch, just like Azalea.

"How do I find someone? What do I look for?" He felt desperate for her council.

"Someone cruel. Someone who reeks of power. Look at the woman a man walks with; her demeanor will tell you everything if you have the eye for it. That will be the kind of man who wants such a curse," Azalea suggested. "Go into town today and survey, but do not get too close. It may take some time before you find someone of this particular breed."

"And then what?" Matthias sat down on the second stair, feeling defeated by the insurmountable task before him.

Juniper studied him before answering. "Tell him you have a business proposition and ask him to come here. We will take it from there."

Matthias left for the market with a list of items Azalea needed and the determination to find someone to take on his curse. It seemed unfathomable that someone would want such a burden, but he hoped to find someone. His mind drifted to the pack that attacked him, how the wolf stared at him just like a human might have, watching his prey suffer. He wondered what kind of person was behind that wolf but couldn't imagine the sort. That was, unfortunately, the exact kind of person he needed to find.

He carried a handful of items through the market as he studied the crowd. To his surprise, the townsfolk didn't recognize him. His hair was shorter now, and he had grown out of his boyish features. His neatly trimmed beard certainly helped, as well. The tension knotted up in his neck and shoulders released. For now, he was safe to peruse.

He knew finding a candidate would not be easy, and to find the right man on the first day was far too optimistic. When he glanced up at the nearest cart of goods, he spotted an odd-looking crow; it was nearly double its regular size. His mother's familiar peered down at him with beady black eyes. Aegidius, he recalled, was the creature's name.

Distracted, he wandered through the market, his boots sinking into the muddy ground, trampled by dogs, children, and carts. The atmosphere was robust, especially for late autumn. The harvest must have been a good one this year, he thought. It brought back the few good memories Matthias had of growing up there.

Three young children raced after one another, slamming into him. The first child fell to the ground while the other two laughed and giggled, pointing at their friend, now covered in dirt.

Matthias extended his hand and assisted the skinny boy to his feet. "Watch where you are going now."

The boy nodded and darted off to play with his friends.

When Matthias looked up again, he saw a woman staring at him.

With big doe eyes and her brown hair neatly pinned back except for one strand that fell over her cheek, she looked more like a work of art or a statue than a real person. But it was her uncanny resemblance to someone Matthias once knew that froze him in place. He felt as though he was sinking into the mud. A basket hung in the crook of her arm, and her head tilted to the side as she studied him.

He was awestruck by the woman, a ghost from his past.

6

SILVANIA

THE YEAR OF THE MOON

RED

With a deep, restorative breath, Red entered her home. The door opened without a sound, despite the age of the house; it had been in the family for generations. Unlike her grandmother's house, it remained well-kept from when the family had money. Her father took pride in maintaining the property and farm on his own, boasting to anyone who would listen about how he managed everything without a son to help. Red had her chores, but collecting eggs and milk was hardly difficult. Perhaps she would have offered to help him with other things if he was not such a sour man.

In her father's eyes, women were only good for cooking and bearing children. She smiled when she thought of how Alina, Sorin, Tatiana, and Lilianna did so much more than that behind the backs of the townsfolk. They were taking back what was theirs. The power blooming in the Earth was for all, but many feared it. Its enticing lull beckoned to Red with a curling finger.

Only the fire greeted her with warmth. From the kitchen, she heard noises—a clatter following a gruff voice.

"It is our only option, Maria," her father said to her mother. "Cristian Fischer has held the title of mayor for too long. What has he done for us? Imagine what I could do with that kind of power."

"What you're suggesting is forbidden," her mother replied.

"No one will dare overthrow me."

"But Rose—"

What does this have to do with me? Red wondered as she closed the door, shutting out the evening air that welcomed itself inside.

"You are not too old to bear me more children." He stopped abruptly. "What was that?"

Only moments later, her father was in sight, barrelling down the hallway toward her. Red braced herself as fear took hold.

He grabbed her wrist, bringing it above her head. Her shoulder threatened to come out of the socket. The new hurt took away from the old; knees and cheeks. Red's eyes widened in terror as she remembered the salve on her cheek.

"You're an hour late for dinner," he growled, his breath stinking of ale. "Your mother toiled over it, and you repay her by arriving late and reeking of smoke and...what is this?" His finger smeared the substance on her cheek, and he wrinkled his nose in disgust.

"Who gave this to you?" he demanded.

Red couldn't answer; Grandmother would never have given her a salve.

It didn't take him long to speculate what Red had done. She felt the color drain from her cut-up cheeks. Wincing instinctively, she tugged her arm against his grasp but could not pull free. She wanted to scream, to tell him he was a coward for blaming her for being late when it was his fault. He had attacked her mother which halted her baking and forced Red to leave late. This circle repeated itself time and time again in her life, and she was tired of it.

It will never stop.

There were hundreds of things she wanted to scream. Over the years, they built up and curdled, filling Red with pure, sour hatred for her father. Words she dreamed of saying but never could. No words ever came from her mouth; she was muted by fear. *I wish you were dead.*

"What were you doing out there, Rose?" His voice went dark, a voice Red was all too familiar with.

She caught a glimpse of her mother peering out from the kitchen, a cloth in her shaking hands. Betrayal clouded Red's senses; not even her mother would step in to defend her from him. Red had always been on her own. But maybe she didn't have to be. Thoughts of the girls in the forest entered her mind again, and she could think of only one thing: freedom.

"Answer me!" her father shouted. Spit sprayed from his mouth and landed on Red's shoulder.

"I knelt in front of the fire on a stick," Red stated as firmly as she could manage, but her voice still quivered. It was not a lie. Still, she knew she would get in trouble simply for speaking of his mother's abuse. She would be passing the blame to someone who would never be at fault in his mind.

Red had no excuse for the salve. That and the smoky smell in her hair were enough. The littlest mistake was enough. *No matter what I do, it always ends this way.*

He yanked her hard, dragging her through the hallways to her room. She cast a forlorn glance at her mother as she passed her, begging for help. Her mother looked down at her hands, silent.

Her father threw her into her room, then slammed and locked the door.

Red was shaken, but she smiled, for she was alone. Yes, she would go hungry, but she would not suffer anymore...at least, until the morning. Being left alone was the most merciful punishment. Her fear slowly dissipated, replaced with rage. She stared hard at the door, her hands balling into fists. A part of her wished her father would return so she could tell him what she had been doing out in those woods.

What she would do again as soon as she got the chance to sneak out.

Red crawled into bed and pulled her hair from its messy confines atop her head. She sighed in relief as it fell in tumbles over her shoulders, wavy from being pinned up all day. She leaned against the wall and closed her eyes, thinking about the others in the woods. *Were they really doing witchcraft?* Biting her lip, Red gazed to the window as though she could see them out there, their little fire flickering. *Alina was there earlier, watching me as though she wanted me to join her.*

It was the first time any of those girls ever approached Red in the woods. Sorin said they were expecting her, that she was important to them.

Hopping out of bed, she padded to the window, looking for a sign. Hoping to see Alina there again, calling her over, telling her she had a place with them. But she saw nothing but a sea of darkness.

An hour later, the door unlocked. Her mother entered, a candle in her grasp. The light made shadows dance around the walls as she walked toward the bed and sat at the foot of it.

Red winced when her mother put her hand on her knee. She knew it was supposed to be comforting, but the throbbing ache lingered in her joints.

From under her pinafore, her mother revealed a small heel of bread.

Red swiftly devoured it. The sharp edges of her hunger ebbed. She wiped the crumbs from her chin and bed linens.

"Why, Mama?" Red asked, her childish nature coming forth as it always did when she was alone with her.

"The question is not why, Rose," she told her. "We must look at what he does for us. A roof over our heads, food in our bellies—we are safe from harm. This is simply how it is. We must not question it."

Red searched her face, still struggling to understand how her mother stood by silently as he transferred his abuse from her to her daughter. *Is she simply trying to stay alive, too?*

Red wondered if the other girls went through the same thing within their homes. Did Alina suffer at the hands of her father?

Everyone knew the Floarea family was no different than hers. Rumor had it that it was far worse for Tatiana and Lilianna since their mother died. Then there was Sorin, but no one knew much about her—she only moved there a few months ago, near the edges of town. She was an outcast, never welcomed, and no one knew why she chose to move to such a horrible place.

Her mother took a deep breath as if she had said and done enough. "Get some rest, Rose. I love you."

Red muttered, "I love you, too."

Red rolled onto her side and resumed her stare out the window. Frost crept along the edges of the glass, but she was warm, just as her mother said she was. But she did not have a full belly, and she had not been spared from harm. Red could not blame her for what happened. What could she do? To fight back would be the death of her. To leave with nothing but the clothes on her back would be her demise. Her father had made certain that they had nothing to run to. They would starve to death or freeze; no one would open their doors to them.

She could do nothing but watch.

"You must not fear," her mother said as she rose and walked toward the doorway. "Some part of me always knew I would lose you."

She shut the door, and Red heard it lock, the loud clang of the metal making Red's blood curdle. *What does she mean? Why is she going to lose me?* A chill crept up her spine as she remembered what her grandmother said.

"Don't worry. Justice is coming for you."

7

OCLEAU

THE YEAR OF THE CURSE

MATTHIAS

Recovering from his shock, Matthias pried his eyes away. Seeing a woman who so closely resembled his lost love made every nerve in his body vibrate. She was nearly identical, from the roundness of her button nose to the tinge of pink in her cheeks. Tendrils fell loose from her pinned hair, the rich chestnut brown the only difference between them. She even smelled the same. How was it possible? How could I even tell? Matthias's mind reeled, his hands sweating despite the cold.

He nervously fumbled with his purchase in an unsuccessful attempt to look busy. Matthias knew he had to speak with her, even if there was no way she could be her. As he snuck another glance, their eyes caught, and a gentle smile appeared on her perfectly round face. With bravery he did not possess, the woman approached him.

"You look like you have seen a ghost," she said, "and you dropped one of your packages."

Matthias looked at the muddy ground around his feet and saw the wrapped meat he had bought earlier soaking in the boggy mess. "Damn it," he said under his breath.

He snatched it up and wiped the dirt off of the butcher paper.

Mud from the package transferred to his hands, then from his hands to his trousers. Humiliated by such a terrible first impression, Matthias found himself speechless.

She studied him. "I have not seen you around before. You must be new."

Could it be? His heart caught in his throat before he reminded himself of the cold, hard truth of it all. She was dead and had been for nearly ten years.

Finally finding his voice, Matthias told her, "I have recently returned after many years away."

"And what would bring a man back here?" she asked with an airy laugh.

A week ago, Matthias would have agreed. It was never in his plan after escaping this place to return. Everything in this town reminded him of what he lost: a life he could only live with her. Looking at the woman before him, he wondered if he could take that life back. The woman before him had no husband or child; this was a good sign.

"Nothing important," he lied, his voice hardly a whisper as he shook away thoughts of his past. He stuck out his hand for her to shake. "Apologies for being so brash. My name is Matthias."

Her smile grew, and her eyes lit up with amusement. She reached out to shake his hand and said, "My name is Ana. I must be on my way now, but it was a pleasure to meet you, Matthias. I do hope to see you around more often." With effortless grace, Ana turned to walk away. She glanced over her shoulder, locking eyes with Matthias.

Did he know her, or was his mind playing tricks on him because she looked like her?

His stomach twisted into knots, a feeling he had long forgotten. It had been over ten years since he felt that twist, and he found it both uncomfortable and pleasantly addictive.

Ana turned away again, her fast-paced footsteps squelching in the mud.

Perhaps fate was giving him a second chance. His ailment brought him back here, where a chance encounter with a woman who looked like her occurred. If he played his cards just right, perhaps Ana could fill the space left behind from when she died. And fill the space of someone else... Aside from Juniper, there was one other person he left behind ten years ago—someone he could not care for on his own. The twist in his gut told him to pursue this. If he did everything right, maybe he could have a family again.

"Wait, Ana!" He called, bravery coming back to him at last. She might be my chance to replace what I lost, to help me get what was taken from me.

Ana slowed, looking around at the people surrounding them. Then, as if deciding it was safe, she faced Matthias again. She raised her eyebrows, telling him to go on.

"May I see you again? Soon?" he asked. It was a spontaneous decision, dangerous, too. If Azalea caught scent of this, Ana's life would be in danger, especially since Ana looked so much like her. He tried to swallow; her lack of answer perplexed him, making him feel as though he was about to wake up from a dream where she had returned to him.

Ana dipped her head nervously, like a shy child. "Matthias, I...I should not."

"That is not a 'no,'" he said.

She blushed, then walked towards him and placed her gloved hand in the crook of his elbow. She guided him away from earshot. The town was small enough that word spread like the plague.

"It is not a 'no,'" she admitted, though her voice wavered.

"Then I have a chance?" he asked eagerly.

She looked at him pensively, brown eyes darting around as if to seek out familiar faces who might be listening. It was clear something lurked just underneath, desperate to be released. Finally, after much consideration, she whispered, "Matthias...I am a married woman."

His heart sank, and his expression fell with it. Surely the world would not offer him someone to finally replace her, then taunt him like this. Matthias understood the dangers of a married woman speaking to another man and wished no harm to come to Ana.

"I'm sorry, I've overstepped."

It was her turn to fumble, her hands clenching and her lips pursing. "Though I...I wish I wasn't."

He snapped his head up at this. "May I ask why?"

Matthias realized he'd grown so curious about Ana, he forgot his initial reason for coming to the market. It wasn't for bread, spices, and miscellaneous items for Azalea. She'd suggested he look at women in the market and how they acted around their husbands. He hadn't understood what she meant then, but it made sense now.

Ana flickered a gentle glance towards him, her long lashes fluttering. As she shifted from one foot to the other, her expression danced between worry and something else Matthias thought might have been longing. Her mouth opened to speak, but it appeared she had no more words.

"Does he hurt you?" Matthias asked.

"Oh no," she said. "It was more a marriage of convenience. My parents died around the time my husband arrived in town. I would lose the house if it was not in a man's name within the year of my parents' deaths. I must admit...without him, I would have nothing."

Matthias shifted uncomfortably; though he knew the laws surrounding women owning property, he hadn't considered the issues that could arise. Here was a beautiful young woman, forced to marry someone she hardly knew just to keep a roof over her head, while someone like Azalea could own land simply because people were too scared to take it from her. Conflicted by the taste of his privilege on his tongue, he choked back his words.

"He is kind to me. He does the duties expected of a husband, and I a wife." Her voice carried sadness and a hint of resentment. "But there is no love."

"Do you have children?" Matthias inquired.

She shook her head. "No... I cannot..."

An insidious thought slithered in Matthias's mind, creeping in as though Azalea forced it in there, controlling him like a witch controls a familiar. It's all so perfect, he thought. Too perfect. A woman who looked so much like her, in a marriage she wanted to be freed from, unable to have children of her own... He had the solution to fix her problem and his.

Could her husband be the one to take his curse away? He nearly chuckled out loud at the thought; give the man a curse and take his wife away. It was a thought he should never have allowed to cross his mind. Despite the idea bringing him some hope, he knew it was far too soon to suggest something so strange and forbidden to Ana. He didn't even know her.

She must have realized the same thing, for she pulled her arm away from Matthias. "Oh! I must apologize for all this talk of husbands and marriage. It's wrong of me to tell you all of this. I'm deeply ashamed."

"Ana, you have no reason to be ashamed for wishing life had granted you different circumstances," Matthias told her, gently grabbing her hands. Above them, a glimmer of light broke through the gray morning clouds, bringing the hope of a warm afternoon. The soft hum of the market did little to distract him from Ana.

She looked down, still embarrassed.

Without thinking, Matthias used his other hand to tilt her chin up, so he could look at her. "I may be too bold in suggesting this, Ana, but already you have captivated me. I would do anything you asked of me."

"Matthias—" she began to protest, backing away when she realized people had noticed them.

Matthias also stepped back, scanning the trees and buildings for that malicious crow of his mothers'. When he confirmed that Aegidius was not lurking and waiting to report back to Azalea, he turned back to face Ana.

"I may have a solution to your problem, but it is too dangerous to speak of here. I understand that we have just met, and if you do not feel the same, please tell me. But I feel drawn to you in ways I cannot explain. You remind me of someone." He paused to allow himself a breath to slow down. Scaring her away now with a forwardness so unlike himself was not the right way to approach her. "I may be able to help you escape from your marriage."

She appeared stunned, trying to keep her expression neutral. Nothing on her face gave away what she was thinking. No eyebrows knitting together, no pursing of her lips, not even a drain of color in her cheeks. She mastered being unreadable. Was it a skill learned from being married to someone she does not love?

"I would be willing to explore the possibility," she finally said smoothly, as though she planned the words in that moment of shocked neutrality.

"Meet me at the burial grounds tomorrow at midnight. I'm going to tell you something you may not believe, and if you walk away tomorrow and wish to never see me again, I will understand." He spoke quickly, like a nervous rabbit with its heart beating impossibly fast.

"Tomorrow at midnight," she confirmed.

8

SILVANIA

THE YEAR OF THE MOON

RED

The bedroom door was locked, but that was to Red's advantage. Neither parent believed she would leave her room, so they never checked on her once they locked her in. Though Red had never snuck out—she dared not—tonight was an exception. A frightening thought had crept into her mind after Mama left the room, and she was unable to shake it.

It was said that if someone sacrificed a daughter, they could whisper a simple incantation with the name of the family they wanted dead, and it would be done. Though this curse, this Wolf, had not been used in nearly two hundred years, the threat still lingered. Red heard the stories before bed when she was young, but she was nearly a woman. She stopped believing in the legend a long time ago, believing it was simply a story to scare young children. But now, she was not so sure.

She knew who she could ask.

Clambering out of bed, she donned her red cloak and draped the hood over her head. She tiptoed to the window and hooked her fingers under the heavy lower sash. Her muscles flexed as she fought with a window that hadn't been opened since the weather was warm.

Abruptly, it creaked and opened wide. Red froze at the sound; she would surely be caught. She paused, her ears sharp, but she heard nothing from down the hall where her parents slept.

With an exhale that left fog before her face, Red slipped out of the window and dropped into the backyard. Following the same path she took every other day to bring food to her grandmother, Red battled fear and excitement as her stomach twisted at the thought of being out in the woods, thinking about the Wolf that lurked there—was he watching her now?

Red shook thoughts of the Wolf from her mind, focusing instead on Alina, Sorin, Tatiana, and Lilianna. A pang of elation came each time she recalled where she was headed, followed by the worry that the girls had gone home. Hours had passed since she left them in the forest, but Red was determined. Their offer of friendship and solidarity echoed all the warning signs of a coven. *A sweet siren song to lure me in,* Red thought. Mama always said evil is often shrouded in what we want most. She couldn't deny her desire to have such things.

Warmed by her brisk pace, Red continued down the path until she arrived where Alina first approached her. The soft glow of fire and the sound of a lullaby drew her in like a moth to the flame. Twice she stumbled over roots and rocks, but she was too entranced to wince. Staring at the scene before her, she remained hidden in the trees and watched the four girls dance and chant, their bodies gyrating as though possessed.

Sorin abruptly stopped. "We are not alone, girls."

"She's come back," Lilianna exclaimed, rushing away from the warmth of the fire to grab Red's hands. The young brunette went straight to where Red was hiding, as though she was never hidden at all.

Coaxed into the center of it all, Red was dumbfounded.

"What brought you back?" Alina asked from where she stood on the other side of the fire. Sparks flared from the tops of the flames, soaring over her shoulders and flying dangerously close to her thin blonde hair. She showed no fear of the fire.

Before she could reply, Red noticed the blood on Sorin's hands, dripping from the heart she grasped between them. The red liquid stained her fingertips and up to her wrist as though she had dug through a corpse to remove the organ. Red's own heart hammered hard, fear and regret overwhelming her.

Lilianna noticed. The young girl looked over her shoulder and then laughed. "It's a pig's heart, do not worry!"

"Why do you h-have a pig's heart?" Red managed to ask.

"Protection spells require sacrifice," Sorin replied. Her melodic drawl sent chills down Red's spine.

"What are you protecting yourselves from?"

Lilianna's expression darkened. "Tatiana and I will be protected from our father." Years of anger lurked behind her words.

Red's heart sank. *What happens in the Floarea household is worse than mine,* she thought. *Is there no good in this world?*

"I will be protected from the town," Sorin explained. "Every town I have ever lived in has wanted me dead."

"What about you, Alina?" Red asked softly.

Alina waved her hands over the flames; they licked her fingers but never burned them. Her gaze was distant, tears coating her eyes. Then she snapped back into the present. "I will be protected from love."

"From love?" Red's brows knitted together. "I do not believe there is love in this town."

Alina smiled softly. There was a knowing look in her eye as if she had a secret and knew Red did, too. She cocked her head and asked, "What do you wish to be protected from, Red?"

Red thought of what her mother said to her and what her grandmother threatened her with. She nearly choked as the words clung to her tongue. "The Wolf."

The ground crunched beneath Tatiana's feet. Lilianna let go of

Red's hands and looked at the ground. Alina and Sorin kept their attention on Red.

Stepping around the fire, Alina approached, weaving around Lilianna to get through. She took Red's hands in her own, replacing Lilianna's warmth. Then she kissed Red's left cheek, then her right. "Come."

Together, hand in hand, they approached the fire.

Sorin grabbed Red's other hand. "Has it been enacted?"

"I do not know," Red replied to Sorin's question regarding the curse. "I can only speculate."

"It has not," Alina told them, her voice authoritative. "You would know. But we must act quickly if you believe your life is at risk."

Circling the fire, each girl took her assigned place, all within arms reach of each other. Standing on either side of Red were Alina and Sorin. To Alina's right was Tatiana, and beside her was Lilianna. Alina brandished a small blade, pressed it to her lips, then spoke an incantation. *"Dare praesidium meum sanguinem in me."* Her voice was quiet at first. Then she repeated it louder, *"Dare praesidium meum sanguinem in me!"*

Alina removed the blade from her lips and held out her palm.

Sorin dug something out of her pockets, a powder that smelled of lavender blended with carrion. As Alina sliced open her palm, Sorin sprinkled the powder over her wound.

Alina stepped towards the fire, so close that it reached for her nightgown but could not catch it aflame. Flipping her palm, she held it there and squeezed tight, a mixture of blood and the power dripping into the fire, which turned a red so dark that it appeared black near the base; the rest of it was blood-like.

"Amare," she whispered, then withdrew her hand. White sparks burst from the fire, showering Alina but not burning her.

Lilianna and Tatiana repeated the process together; their whisper, *"Pater."*

When it was Sorin's turn, she put her hand in the fire without hesitation. She growled, *"Silvania."*

When it was Red's turn, she could not grip the blade as Sorin handed it to her—despite wanting to join, wanting to be safe from harm, wanting to be part of this coven. Years of being warned about things just like this rippled through her. *Never stray from the path, never dabble in witchcraft, never open that part of herself up.*

Suddenly, like a flower blooming in spring, Red felt something unfold inside of her, absorbing the power around her. Power from the other girls, power from the Earth itself, as though it was the most natural thing in the world. A thought occurred to Red: *Denying myself this power, am I denying myself what it means to be a woman?*

Sorin's brown eyes narrowed, not in anger but in understanding. "Alina," she beckoned with blood dripping from her hand. "She must be initiated."

Alina wiped her palm on her white dress and turned to face Red head-on. Taking the knife from Sorin's hand, she pressed it against Red's willing hand, which she held gently. A warmth spread from Red's palm to her stomach, making it flip.

"Everything will be okay," Alina whispered.

Red nodded to encourage her to go on, offering a small smile.

Alina dug the blade into Red's flesh.

Flinching, Red stared in awe as her flesh parted, the skin peeling back like a lipless gape, followed by pooling blood. Finally, the pain came, a white-hot sensation that made Red feel alive.

Alina gripped Red's hand, interlocking her fingers to combine their blood. Then Alina pressed her forehead to Red's. "I'm going to kiss you," she whispered. "Is that all right?"

"Yes."

Her lips touched Red's.

Red shivered with pleasure. Was it witchcraft, or was it something more? The question ran through her mind a dozen times before the brief kiss concluded, and Alina released her hand. The tingle on her lips lingered, and Red's stomach lurched as her heart hammered against her ribcage.

Alina stepped out of the way to let Sorin take over, but her gaze never left Red.

Sorin added powder to Red's fresh cut, its heat making her skin prickle. The light blue veins along her wrist darkened to black, and the tingle turned into a dull ache. Warmth crept up from the soil, igniting her body as though she stood within the fire. Beads of sweat formed above her brow. It was not the flame that warmed her, but the Craft. She could feel the forbidden power spread through her body. It built up in her chest, filling her heart with a surge of strength and desire.

Red had watched the other girls do it, and now it was her turn. What she needed to be protected from—was it even real? It didn't matter; what mattered was that she stopped it before anything happened. The word came off her tongue easily, and though she knew nothing of the old language, the word 'wolf' was one uttered by every tongue in their town.

"Lupus," she whispered.

9

OCLEAU

THE YEAR OF THE CURSE

MATTHIAS

Darkness cloaked the town; only a glimmer of the waxing gibbous cast light on the burial grounds. Ancient and broken headstones created ghoulish shadows along the length of the moss-covered ground. Earthy musk filled the air, paired with the smell of an overdue snowfall.

The night air was calm, yet Matthias was still chilled down to the bone despite his warm furs and leathers. He tucked his hands into his pockets and wished he had chosen a different time to meet. Midnight was safest, though, without the chance of someone overhearing.

The snap of a tree limb startled him from his thoughts.

Cloaked in a light brown hood, Ana stepped into the moonlight. Her curious eyes scanned until she spotted him, then she briskly maneuvered through the headstones with such grace that she appeared dreamlike.

The ghost of his past.

"I did not think you would come," Matthias said. Shock rippled through his system. Shock that she decided to show up despite how outlandish his request was.

"I have nothing to lose by coming," she told him, rubbing her arms with her gloved hands.

The lingering feeling of distrust Azalea cursed him with gripped him, despite his desire to believe her. "How did you avoid your husband?"

"He is away," Ana admitted nervously. Her fingers entwined in front of her hips, clutching her skirts. "He will be gone for a week."

Bringing up her husband was easier than he expected, leading to more pressing questions that he needed to have answered. "Before I say more, you must promise that what we discuss will stay between us," Matthias said.

Ana unclasped her hands and grasped Matthias's. "You can trust me."

Matthias wanted to melt into her touch. Already the possibility of rebuilding what he lost seized his mind; Ana fit the part. However, her resemblance to his lost love meant she would be unsafe should Azalea discover her.

He already knew he wanted to protect Ana, to care for her, and to eventually love her. He knew she was looking for freedom, but he had one more thing she might want. "If this works, and you gain freedom from your husband, where will you go? You said you married to keep your land, a roof over your head, but without him—"

Ana cut Matthias off. "Does this plan of yours involve murdering my husband?"

"No," Matthias told her, though it felt like a lie.

When Ana said no more, shifting on her feet as she watched him, Matthias continued. "Tell me what you want."

Their eyes locked for a moment, and the shared gaze warmed Matthias. Ana took a shaky breath, the air fogging before her. She pressed her gloved fingers to her lips, puzzled by the question; it was clear that no one had ever asked her what she wanted.

"To leave Ocleau," she finally said. "To go far away from this place, maybe even see the world. I have been tied down here my whole life;

I've lost everyone I have ever cared about here. I have no family left. I want it all behind me." Her hands waved with her words when she spoke as though she plucked her desires right from the air, snatching them like fragments of a dream.

"You've left town. You've been further than its borders... Perhaps you could aid me."

Her words were powerful and precisely what Matthias wanted to hear. Concern forced its way into his mind. *Is this too good to be true?*

He wanted to be part of her dream, and he could offer her the chance to escape—and a family—if she so chose. It meant betraying Azalea; if she even suspected Matthias planned to run off with Ana after she freed him from the curse, she would kill her without hesitation.

"Are you familiar with witchcraft?" Matthias asked abruptly.

Ana cringed at the thought, then replied sourly, "I know it can lead to death, either caused by the Craft or by those who disapprove of it."

Her answer did not satisfy Matthias. "I also disapprove of it. I wish there was no such thing as witchcraft. However, my life depends on it now."

Her shuffling to keep warm abruptly stopped, and she eyed Matthias curiously. She wrapped her arms around her body to prevent the cold from seeping in and stepped enough to touch him. She reached her hand up and placed it against his chin. Her smooth goatskin gloves were warm, and he fought the urge to lean into the palm of her hand. If he closed his eyes, he could imagine *her*.

"You are Matthias Luca, are you not?" she asked as she stepped back.

He stood straight, then cautiously nodded. *Has she known all along?* Matthias knew people might recognize him when he returned to Ocleau, and there was a chance they might cast him out for what they believed he did. Doubt entered his mind, encroaching on rational thought; perhaps Ana tricked him with her uncanny looks. *Did she have a sister?* Matthias wondered. *No, she grew up in an orphanage.*

Perhaps she lured him out into the night as vengeance for something he did not do.

A soft smile danced on her lips, disappearing as fast as it came.

"And?" he asked.

"There are rumors you drowned your last lover." Ana sounded confident but not entirely accusatory. Something had flipped in her voice; she no longer appeared like an oppressed woman seeking refuge.

Matthias stiffened, grimacing as he thought back to when *she* died when he found her face down and bloated in the water. "I never harmed her," he replied through gritted teeth.

None of his plans would proceed if Ana believed he killed her.

"But someone did," Ana said.

"I believe it was my mother." Matthias decided being honest with Ana was his best choice. No more lies, not to anyone but Azalea. "Ana, I have something inside of me that will destroy me. More than losing her did."

"You can't even say her name," Ana said, bemused.

Matthias wondered if she grew up in the orphanage with her but recalled Ana mentioning her family home, and knew that wasn't right. He couldn't put his finger on it.

"Riina," he whispered shamefully. He lowered his head. "Losing Riina."

When he found the courage to look back up, she was staring right through him, as if waiting for him to continue.

Shakily, he said, "On the full moon, I will become a werewolf unless my mother can take the curse inside of me and put it into someone else."

"That is where my husband comes in," she breathed.

"A strong enough person can control it, even live with it. Tell me, Ana, if he was inflicted with this, would he make you leave Ocleau to keep you safe? Or would he flee?"

She nodded warily. "One or the other, yes."

"The final piece is where it becomes difficult," Matthias continued. "Your husband must be willing to take my curse."

The way Ana looked at him made him feel as though she could read every thought that ran through his mind. With only her eyes, she peeled back every layer of flesh until she found the bones, the blood, the veins, the organs. She cracked through his ribcage and found his heart; he hoped she knew his intentions were pure. When she lowered her gaze, she pressed her hands to her own heart as if she were doing the same to herself, feeling for what she truly wanted, weighing the risk and the reward. As if trying to decide if it was worth giving up her mundane, yet safe, life for an unpredictable one with Matthias.

"Can you promise me that if I help you with this, you will help me leave Ocleau?" she asked.

The words he so desperately wanted to hear slammed into him. Even though she spoke nothing of remaining with him once they left, it was enough for him to agree. "I promise."

"Then we have a week to figure out how to make my husband want your curse."

10

SILVANIA

THE YEAR OF THE MOON

RED

When the pig's heart sizzled out, and the fire faded into nothing but a whisper, the night ended. Although it was early in the evening, and the girls still had hours of darkness ahead of them, their goal had been accomplished. Energy vibrated through the forest, pulsing with more power than gale-heavy winds. Each girl could feel it, the life emanating from the trees and earth around them reaching up through their roots to whisper their knowledge.

Sorin was the first to speak, startled out of her daze when Lucien clambered over her shoulder and perched on his hind legs. He tucked his front paws into his chest, his little claws twitching ever so slightly. Sorin absentmindedly reached her hand up and stroked his brown fur. "Let us be protected and never harm one another."

"We are all we have in this world," Alina added quietly. "We must look out for one another. Protect each other."

Red realized Alina spoke to her and quickly became alert. All the other girls already knew their place—they were expected to always look out for each other. She assumed Tatiana and Lilianna had done so since they were born. But for an outsider like Red to witness what she had and be included, the ground rules needed to be laid out before her.

"Do you swear to remain silent about what happens here?" Sorin asked.

Red nodded; they were the first people in Red's whole life who had ever extended a welcoming hand or lifted her when she fell. They showed her kindness in a world full of cruelty. Witches they may be, but Red knew now that witches were not the horrid things she was raised to believe. "I will never betray your trust," she promised.

"I will walk Red home," Alina offered.

Red was flooded with relief. She was scared to part from the glowing embers of the fire and the beautiful faces of her peers. With Alina by her side, Red felt safe for the first time in her life. *I was told never to stray in fear of what lurked in the woods,* she thought, *but what lurks outside these woods is far scarier.* She suspected that unity between girls was a frightening thought to the men who ran the town.

"We have been doing this for a long time and have never been caught," Alina said, pulling Red from her thoughts. She linked her arm with Red's, the smooth crook of her elbow soft against her skin. She placed her other hand on Red's arm. "I trust what happened here tonight will remain a secret."

"I will never speak of it," Red answered honestly. "What would I gain in betraying the trust of my first friends? If that is what I can call you..."

"Friends, sisters, witches," Alina spoke in a sing-song voice. "Call me what you need."

Red's cheeks burned despite the cold air.

Above them, trees loomed, their tops hanging down like giants craning their necks to see the ants below. No birds flew this late at night or this deep into the winter, yet a large raven was perched, watching them curiously. She could still feel its eyes following her as they walked, studying her every move. Red was unable to shake the ominous feeling and tightened her grip on Alina.

"Why did you ask to be protected from love?" Red asked, her eagerness to know showing in her haste. "In a town so devoid of it, why would you wish to be hidden away from what little you might find?"

"Did you know Tatiana and Lilianna's father loves his daughters a bit too much?" Alina asked.

"There are rumors," Red admitted, ashamed she had heard what Mr. Floarea did to his daughters, but no one ever stepped in to stop him. The villagers believed it wasn't their place to determine what went on in a household other than their own.

"Tell me, Red, do your parents love you?"

"My father? No. My mother?" Red paused to think. It was not an easy answer after what happened only a few hours ago. Years of suffering while her mother looked away made Red think maybe she did not love her. She shook her head, ridding herself of these thoughts. Surely someone had to love her.

"I do believe she loves me," she said, hopeful that saying the words aloud would help her truly believe them.

They drew closer to town, dark in the absence of glowing fires as the townsfolk slumbered in their warm beds. The moon still hung low in the sky. Red would ache tomorrow from the beating she received from Grandmother and would be tired from staying out all night, but she would sacrifice her sleep any time if it meant spending more time with Alina and the others. With them, Red had even forgotten about her pain.

"And what has love gotten you?" Alina continued.

"Nothing." Red breathed the word, which clung to the air before her in the fog of breath before dissipating into nothing.

Alina and Red stopped just before they crossed over the town line. For the first time, Red saw a strange aura surrounding the town as though hundreds of years of hatred soured the air. Beyond the town line was the feeling of freedom, but it came with fear. Fear of the unknown, offered by the girls in the woods. Fear of the Wolf, whom she dreaded she soon would meet. Fear of being unprotected. Red looked down at her hands and noticed they were no longer shaking; she was not scared of Alina. If she went back to the woods and the Coven, she knew she would feel protected and be protected.

"I'll admit I feel love too quickly. Too deeply. I no longer wish to feel it because I know it leads to nothing but pain," Alina said. "I am different, and if the town knew it, I would be cast out."

"Different how?" Red asked, longing to hear the words. Like the air she needed to breathe, she needed those words. If they were made physical and she could reach out to touch them, she would know what she felt inside was real.

Alina smiled with a sadness so deep, it seemed it would never be removed entirely. As if, whether she was free from ever feeling love or if she felt it so profoundly that it consumed her, she would always look saddened. The delicate girl with white-blonde locks broke from Red's gaze and held her hands, their paleness glowing in the moonlight. Red knew Alina would not reveal how she was different, how she loved differently, yet deep down she knew why.

Because she felt it too.

"Goodnight, Red. Think about me in the dead of night." Alina kissed Red's cheek just below the cuts, then slunk back into the darkness. Her ghostly form seemed to float away until she was too far to be seen by the naked eye.

Red whispered long after she disappeared, "Goodnight, Alina."

Azalea

Juniper

Matthias — Rum

Elise

PART II
The Case

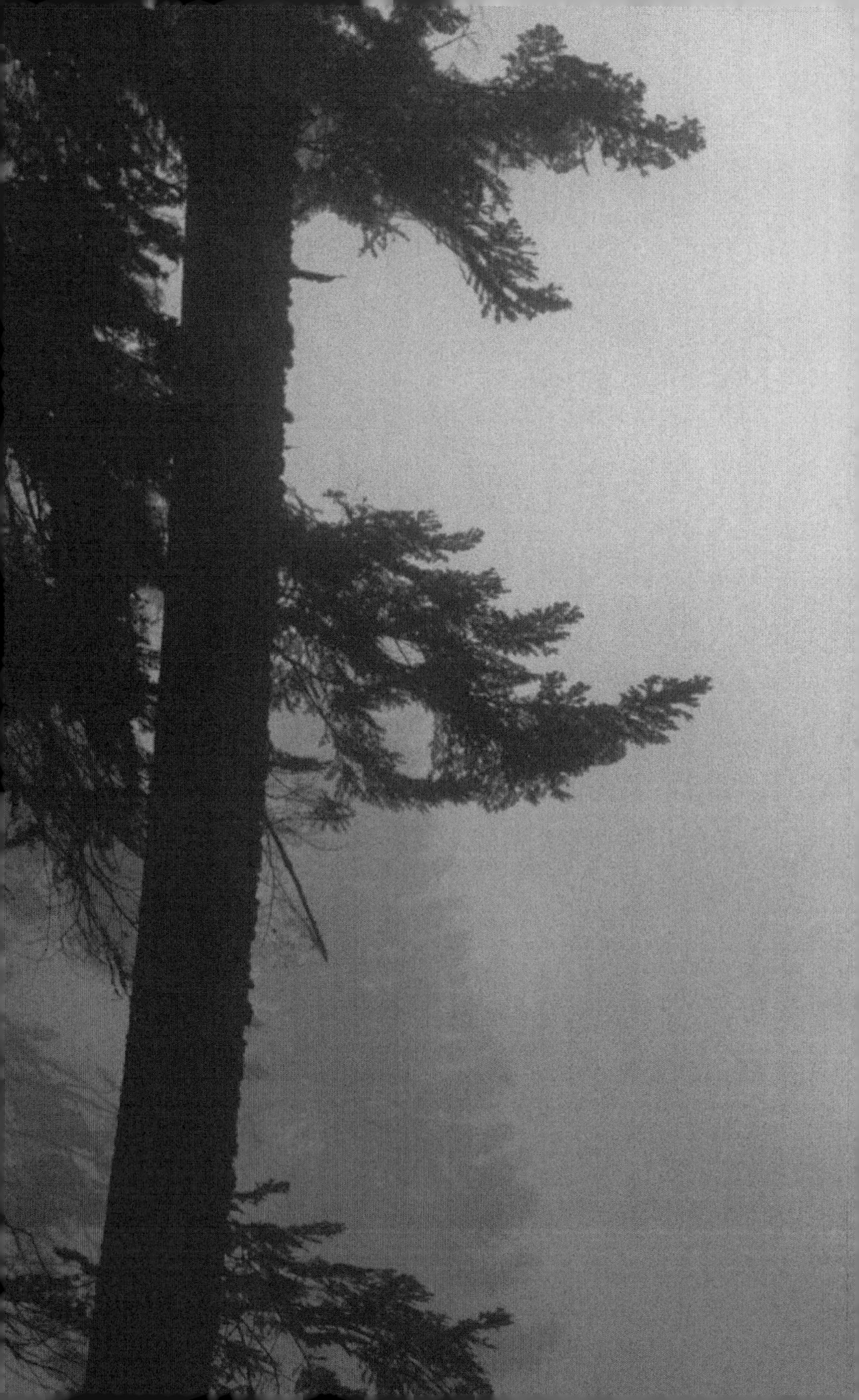

11

SILVANIA

THE YEAR OF THE MOON

RED

A scream of a chicken outside forced Red to open her eyes. *Father is already up—I'm late for my morning chores.*

Unexpectedly alive and still draped in the warmth of her new friendships, she sat up and stretched in her bed. Having survived the long night in the brutal cold while dipping her hands in the forbidden pools of witchcraft, she felt the power coursing through her. She wasn't sure how she managed to slip back in through her window, disrobe and change into a new nightgown, shoving the smoke-scented one deep underneath her bed; her memory was shrouded in mist. Now, underneath the down duvet, Red felt every bone and joint ache as the adrenaline faded from her system. But for the first time in her short life, she experienced joy.

The powers of the Craft are forbidden, she thought, as she took inventory of her aches and pains. *But maybe the power was worth the risk.*

She got out of bed on tired legs, then crouched down and reached for her crumpled nightgown. When she pulled it out, she smelled the smoke and earthiness, sending a jolt of happiness through her. Red stood back up a new woman. Everything felt different, from the faint soot smell on her flesh to the tiredness in her bones. Donning her warmest clothes, as though to fight off the phantom cold from the night before, she went to the door and grabbed the handle—it was still locked.

Her heart sank. With the sun already rising, it was a late start to begin with. Why would she still be locked in? Red knocked gently on the door to remind her mother she was still there. Moments later, it unlocked with a faint click. No one opened the door on the other side, so Red gingerly did it herself and stepped into the vacant hallway. With silent, stocking-clad feet, Red followed the smell of warm bread and found herself in the doorway of the kitchen.

"Good morning, Mama," Red said politely, trying to keep the edge from her voice that would reveal her anger at being locked in her room. It was not the first time, but after what her mother and grandmother said to her, it was different. Now, being locked in could mean they were planning something...something that could cause her great harm.

She brushed off the previous night's imprisonment. Her fear of being sacrificed to the Wolf was dwindling, deflating into almost nothing. She need not worry; she was protected now. Satisfied, she waited for her mother to instruct her, but she didn't turn her attention from the bread she was kneading. She didn't look up, or even bother to brush back the hair that fell from her bonnet.

"Would you like me to fetch the eggs?" Red asked, needing something to do before anxiety consumed her. "If the hens have laid any, that is."

"I already gathered them, Rose," her mother replied sharply. Her cheeks were red from exertion.

Red decided to use this to her advantage. "If I am not needed for chores, may I go out today?"

Her mother looked up, and Red saw dark shadows surrounding her red eyes; she had been crying. With a flour-coated hand, she waved Red off and returned to kneading the bread so fiercely Red knew it would not rise. The flat loaf would be tossed to the pigs, and she would face her husband's wrath.

Turning on her heel, Red darted back into her room to grab her hood and was out of the house before her mother could change her mind. She snatched the empty basket and headed to the woods to forage. The moment the brisk air hit her skin, she felt blood rushing to her cheeks. Tears infringed on her vision, and the unavoidable runny nose showed up, but she never felt more alive than she did then. Surviving a night when she could have been caught practicing witchcraft—the punishment for such being burned alive or crushed by rocks—and having avoided being sacrificed to the Wolf, she felt invincible.

In the course of a single night, Red had friends. Sisters, Alina said she could call them. Unity felt powerful. *Not just friends, protectors.* Having always been at the receiving end of a slap or a shove, simply the knowledge that she was protected from being sacrificed gave her comfort. *I hope they know what they are doing.*

Lost in thoughts of wolves and spells, Red found herself walking by Alina's home. She glanced conspicuously into the windows in hopes of catching her friend's attention. When no movement inside suggested anyone was home, Red kept on walking. Around the corner, she bumped right into the blonde, gasping as she did.

"Red," she breathed her name. "What brings you here?"

Red had no answer, not one that she could speak aloud. Her heart tried to answer, thumping so hard Red was certain Alina could hear it.

"Are you gathering?" Alina asked, head tilting towards the basket in Red's hands.

"Y-yes," Red stammered.

"May I join you?" Alina asked, and when Red nodded, she hooked her arm. She guided Red towards the forest, stepping over the town line and into the woods.

Red stayed quiet, enjoying her company as they half-heartedly foraged. "I saw you yesterday," Red said vaguely.

Alina laughed. "Did you think it was all a dream?"

"No," Red stammered. "Not last night, I mean earlier. B-before I left my house, you were there…"

Alina nodded, glancing at the path before them when Red turned to look at her.

Red had never before sensed Alina's shyness, but it was clear now. She was always a quiet girl, not rowdy like the Floarea sisters, never a troublemaker. And yet, she was a witch.

"Yes, I was," Alina admitted. "Did you know that every woman is born with a draw to the Craft? Some men too, but not as many."

Red shook her head, slowing her walk to watch Alina's body language as she spoke.

"We all have it in us, and I can sense it is very strong in you." Alina stopped to study her face. The coldness soaked into them as they stood between the trees. "I could feel it in you. I've felt it for a long time. But that is not the only reason I find myself walking by, hoping to…to catch your eye."

They both remained silent as Alina's words hung between them.

Then, at last, as she began to put the pieces together, Red said, "Last night, you said… You said that the way you love, the town would not agree with." Red turned to face Alina, hand on her forearm to hold her steady. With pleading eyes, she asked, "What did you mean?"

Alina smiled. She brushed a strand of hair from Red's face, pushing it behind her ear. The gentle touch sent sparks through Red, but she remained motionless as if any movement would scare Alina away like a deer. Then, Alina kissed her; a soft kiss, much like the night before, around the fire, only sweeter without anyone watching. Their lips fit perfectly. Alina's were warm and smooth, while Red's were dry and inexperienced.

Overhead, a raven watched them unnoticed.

When Alina broke away, her eyes were cast downwards. "They do not understand, and people fear what they do not understand."

"I..." Red stammered, touching Alina's cheek and lifting her face to look at her. "I understand."

"If anyone finds out..." Alina whispered, trailing off.

"They won't." Red felt bold. The kiss empowered her. Witchcraft empowered her. "You're protected, hopefully not from... *all* love... They won't find out because I will not let them."

Alina looked right into Red's soul. "I won't let the Wolf take you."

"Let him take me if we cannot be together," Red whispered.

Smiling, Alina kissed her again.

∽

A fortnight passed, and Red forgot about the Wolf. Swept up in her newfound friendships and what she began to consider love, Red's confidence grew. They did not meet every evening, and when she saw neither her Coven nor Alina, she found herself walking home alone from her grandmother's nurturing a growing hatred for her family. Very little had changed in her life, but Red had changed.

As she made her way home, darkness fell. Without her friends by her side, Red did not feel as assured the woods wouldn't reach out for her with long tendril-like branches and pull her in forever. The moment she crossed the town line, she felt as close to relaxed as she could. The lanterns outside the few homes she passed were lit—a sign to the children that they should be home. Mud squelched beneath her shoes; they would need a good washing when she got home.

Leaping over a puddle from the rain three days before, she landed with both feet and looked ahead to see where she was going. Her home in the distance was hard to see, with only one window showing any sign of light. A single candle lit a whole room, as if someone was trying to keep their actions a secret.

Red cocked her head to the side. *It is only suppertime, why were there no other lights on?* Suddenly the door opened, though neither parent appeared. There was nothing in the darkness of the open doorway, and Red stepped backward into the puddle she had leaped over.

Though she could see nothing, Red felt the energy creeping toward her like a gust of wind. It was not like the power she felt from the Earth, but something evil. As it crept closer, blowing out the lanterns as it flew by, Red froze, unable to move a muscle.

The invisible energy hit her hard in the chest, spreading through her veins like sharp needles, starting from her core, expanding through her limbs, and out through her fingers. It lodged itself inside her body, attaching to her like a parasite, and Red's eyes rolled back in her head. Her head fell backward at a painful angle, her spine bending, her hands extending out to the side. She convulsed, then closed in on herself, her head snapping forward so she faced the ground. She could not scream, despite the pain and terror. Her shoulders were hunched, her knees bent like a feral beast; her back heaved with heavy breaths.

Then she stood, drawing herself up to her full height, turning around and striding toward the forest with a bewitched gait. Unable to stop herself, knowing she had been sacrificed, Red could not even weep.

12

OCLEAU

THE YEAR OF THE CURSE

ANA

Ana sat on her bed in her modest two-bedroom home, passed down for generations in her family. She scanned the empty log walls. The lack of personalization mimicked her life: empty. Her family was gone, her husband did not count, and she would have no children.

Looking down at her belly, she winced. She knew she would not carry on the family line; it would die with her. Being barren was not the worst thing for Ana, though she knew many women saw it as a curse and suffered a deep, impenetrable sadness because of it. Ana saw it as a gift, for she saw too many women die during birth and too many babies die before their first year—winter killed more than illness. She never wanted Blaez's child.

Finally, she rose and dressed, donning a thick brown skirt and simple white blouse. Then she brushed her hair, leaving it loose. After feeding the livestock, tending to the fire, and making herself something to eat, Ana set out to find Matthias. She was worried people would talk if they saw them together again, but she had no choice. She needed someone with power to start them down this dangerous path. That someone was Azalea Luca.

Matthias was easy to find at the market, his tall, burly stature similar to Blaez's. She immediately gravitated towards him when she spotted him, but stopped before she looked too obvious. She pretended to smell soaps and consider the small selection of fruits being sold. She kept herself occupied for an appropriate time, then decided to make contact in a subtle way. Surrounded by townsfolk, gossip would spread like wildfire if anyone thought they were having an affair.

What we are doing is so much worse.

She walked up to the cart where Matthias stood, feeling an apple for bruises. She joined him in studying the quality of the fruit, palming her own apple to feel its firmness.

"I have an answer," Ana whispered, keeping her voice low enough that the nearby merchant could not hear her. "We should speak in private."

"The cemetery?" he asked. He grabbed another apple and squeezed it gently, then tossed it in the basket he carried.

Ana shook her head. "Somewhere more private. My home."

With tense shoulders, Matthias paid the merchant for the fruit and headed off to another booth. As they strolled along, not quite side by side but close enough to speak, Matthias brought up the obvious. "That is very dangerous, not only for the both of us but for what might become of this town if I do not break free from this..." he trailed off.

The word 'curse' would turn a few heads. Matthias looked up at the sky, scanning the trees and the tops of the merchant carts, then looked relieved. Ana wondered what he was looking for; in the meantime, she glanced at faces, hoping no one would recognize her.

"He will not return." Ana knew Blaez's habits and patterns well enough.

"When?" Matthias asked. "When should I be there?"

Ana bought a bar of soap, the cost making her stomach clench in protest, but she needed to leave with something. All around them, townsfolk she recognized glanced over at the duo, whispers already starting to arise. Though she herself was often reclusive at best, Matthias was a face that sparked conversation. Even ten years after Riina's death and his departure, she worried he would once again be the talk of the town. The infamy would do them no good. They could not meet in public again.

She slipped the soap into her skirt pocket and smiled at the merchant but didn't look at Matthias again. The whispers grew louder, so she told Matthias, "Stay in the market for another quarter hour, purchase one more item, then take the long way around town. I live on a small acreage at the west end. I will leave a flower on my doorstep."

Without another word, Matthias strolled along to another booth while Ana deftly moved back in the direction of home. Arriving at her door fifteen minutes later, she plucked a winter rose from the garden. She placed it on the doorstep and noticed blood on the stem. Turning over her finger, she saw the blood beading and dripping from it, this time landing on the white petals. Surprised that she did not feel it, she stuck her finger in her mouth, the coppery flavor making her grimace.

She headed inside, disappearing into the warmth. Anxiously, she awaited the knock on the door. To distract herself, she boiled water for some tea over the fire. The hot drink steamed before her, the heat seeping through the clay mug and singeing her fingertips. *Despite everything happening—Matthias, Blaez, moon curses, witchcraft—I'm prepared for anything that comes my way.*

The knock came a half hour later, and she darted to the door after placing the mug on the table. Matthias greeted her with a nervous smile, the discomfort of being in another man's home, alone with his wife, etched onto his face. He did nothing to hide it. That was the difference between men and women—women could hide everything if they wished, taught at an early age that they had to listen, be obedient, and accept what they had. *Matthias must hate the fact that he wants a woman who is already married.*

"Tell me," Matthias demanded softly, his voice more desperate than commanding.

Ana saw how hopeless he was and faltered for a second. She appreciated this; he needed her. She beckoned for him to sit in one of the chairs surrounding the hearth, the warmth of the fire reaching out its hands and guiding them along like the pied piper. She took a seat, forgetting about her tea, and felt a nervous twist in her stomach. *If this doesn't work, I will have nothing left. Matthias will be cursed, and I will be trapped here.*

"Your mother, she is well-known for her skills in witchcraft. She must have a skillset in potions and tonics, yes?" Ana asked, revealing her minimal knowledge of witchcraft.

"I do not doubt it." Matthias nodded. "She has phials, tonics... there is always something awful brewing in her cauldron."

"Then she will be capable of making me appear ill, yes?" Ana leaned forward in her seat, only inches away from Matthias.

Matthias frowned, his thick eyebrows pinching together. "I believe so... But Ana, how will this help?"

She raised a palm, fingertips still red from concocting the tea. "Blaez will return in a few days. When he returns, I will appear seriously ill. If I have gauged my husband correctly, he will seek a healer. We have little coin but not enough to spare for a doctor. It is my understanding your mother does not exclusively take coin but is willing to barter or trade, as well. A gentle suggestion from me, and he will go to her."

"In exchange for your life, he will give his..." Matthias trailed off, unconvinced.

"Yes," Ana confirmed. "He would do anything I asked of him."

Matthias tensed, leaning back in the chair so he was not so close to Ana. His fingers folded together in his lap as he considered her suggestion. Blaez was the best chance he had at getting the curse out of him. A sudden, deep sigh came from his lips, and he shook his head. "No, it's not enough."

"Not enough?" Ana repeated.

"This is Azalea we are talking about. She won't buy it for a second. She won't understand why you want to leave a husband so devoted to saving your life."

"Then I'll tell her I wish to leave this town, to be free of my husband. As a woman, she should understand."

Matthias stood up and walked to the window overlooking the fields. His fingers spread like spiderwebs against the sill as he leaned into his hands. Turning again, this time leaning against the window, he told Ana, "I have no doubt she will think you have fallen in love with me, and I... And I, with you. If we have something between us, if she even has an inkling of that, be it true or not, she will realize that I would want to leave to keep us both safe. She will not let me leave her again."

Ana kept her face composed and calculated, giving nothing away. "Then we will say he beats me and that I need to escape for my life."

"Tell me, Ana," he said as he pushed himself off the window frame, "Then why would he sacrifice his life for yours?"

"The curse is not death; the curse is power. The power-hungry will kill for such a curse; they consider it a gift. Your mother will believe Blaez will want both—to keep me alive and to have that power."

He nodded as he grasped her idea. Ana knew it would work so long as they both played their parts well enough to fool Azalea. Matthias's eyes revealed his grief, the loss of Riina still eating away at him like maggots under the skin. It was easy to see he was already infatuated with her. Ana could see it the moment he laid eyes on her because she looked so much like Riina. This likeness put a target on her back; Azalea would believe what she wanted to believe.

I can be convincing enough to trick her.

"She will need proof," Matthias choked out the sentence.

Ana rose from her chair, brushing non-existent crumbs from her skirts, and stood an arm's length away from Matthias. He smelled of herbs and spices, the essence of witchcraft absorbed in the fabric of his clothing. Ana made sure to meet his eyes so her words would be stronger, to show that she would not back down. "Hit me."

Matthias gaped. "H-hit you?"

"Enough to leave a bruise. On my shoulder, then grip my wrist and pull it hard enough to leave marks." Ana turned around and braced herself for the blow.

"No, I will not... I cannot hit a woman," Matthias managed.

She glanced over her shoulder. "I can do it myself if you are not able. The mantle above the fireplace would work to create a bruise, but it would be less believable."

Ana knew the best way to get a man to do something he did not want to do was to make him feel inferior. It worked on Blaez often enough, though he never laid a hand on her.

A sigh came from Matthias. "Ana..."

"Do it," she snapped. She felt the stinging pain of a fist contacting her shoulder. She stumbled forward with a shout of agony; she had never been hit before. The shock passed, but the pain lingered.

In an instant, Matthias's pleas of apology came, begging for her forgiveness. She turned with a slow grace and rolled up her sleeve, holding her left arm out. She wasn't sure if she could lift her right arm now that her shoulder throbbed so hard. Matthias held her wrist, and his eyebrows knitted together as if he were the one being hurt. Shutting his eyes, he twisted and yanked in one swift movement, pulling Ana towards him.

She yelped as she collapsed into him, vibrating with excitement. Matthias instinctively wrapped his arms around her frame.

"I am so sorry," he said, his face anguished. "I am so sorry."

Ana smiled against his spice-scented, broad chest. It was the first time she had felt anything in a long time.

13

SILVANIA

THE YEAR OF THE MOON

ALINA

Alina used the glow from the moonlight to see, for the candle beside her did little. The moon called to her like an old friend, reminding her of times she spent beneath it, dancing and singing, learning the ways of the Earth and how to harness the energy it held. Such energy came from the roots of the trees, full of ancient knowledge. Another kind of power came from the moon. The moon created waves in the oceans; the tides obeyed every command it gave. She could feel each change as it waxed and waned.

Alina used that powerful light to create a potion to curb the effects of her insomnia. She had suffered sleepless nights since childhood, which made her days drag on, leaving dark circles under her eyes and weakness in her body. The meager hours that she did manage to rest were fitful and filled with nightmares.

One day, she decided to embrace the night since it so desperately wanted her awake throughout its hours. Combining herbs, liquids, and the right amount of mixing, she found a way to alert her senses. She discovered a love for the night and everything that came with it. In tune with the moon more than the sun, the soft sounds of nocturnal creatures in the woods had always beckoned her. She bathed in the energy of the forest, the energy of the moon, and her black skies. Alina found her calling that night.

A few months later, Sorin arrived in the town with more knowledge of witchcraft than Alina ever thought possible. She told Alina that while something drove her out of her own home, something much stronger brought her to Silvania. A power capable of drawing her across oceans.

Since Sorin arrived, she taught Alina everything she knew. Together they grew and bonded, using their collective intuition and connection with nature to enhance their abilities. They made it their goal to help other girls in similar situations, young women who suffered at the hands of their parents or siblings. Especially those with an aptitude for witchcraft who did not know how to harness it or realize what it was. Like Red. She was a natural witch with a gift, yet she never embraced the energy of nature. It came as no surprise to Alina; the town snuffed out women's power wherever it could.

Alina added her concoction to a cup of water and watched it swirl into the clear liquid, turning it gray with a hint of purple. She focused on the glass, but something moving outside her window shifted her attention. Nothing stirred this late in the evening unless there was trouble: an angry man with a mind full of vengeance, a jealous spouse spiteful of a lover.

A young woman in a red hood.

Jumping up from where she crouched, Alina ignored the cry of her muscles, which had been locked in one position for so long they had seized. She shoved the window open, knocking over the freshly brewed potion. She paid it no mind. Herbs could be replaced; people could not.

She hopped out her window and landed softly in the grass below. Each blade of grass sent energy through the soles of her feet as nature wrapped itself around her in cold bliss. Hoping the strength and power stayed with her, she pursued Red through the forest. Her posture was wrong, too proper... Alina's head spun as she realized what had happened.

Red had been sacrificed to the Wolf. A family would die tonight.

"Red!" Alina hissed. The last thing she needed was to attract the attention of the whole town. Her own parents did not worry her, though she didn't know what sort of punishment they would inflict upon her if she was discovered. She always suspected they would understand or pretend they never discovered it in the first place. Just as they turned a blind eye to how she loved, she suspected they turned a blind eye to her witchcraft to keep her safe. Stories of witches being burned were not so old that they were forgotten.

"Red!" she called again, daring to raise her voice a little louder.

Just when she thought Red would drop her stony demeanor, she turned sharply and cut through Alina's family garden.

Alina raced to her friend, thankful Red turned into her yard and not someone else's. Her bare feet padded hard against the cartwheel-ruined path before she darted to her garden. When she caught up, Alina gripped Red's arm tightly and yanked her, hoping to pull her out of her trance.

Red's trudge did not falter. Though Alina pulled with all her might, whatever force of nature compelled her was stronger than anything she had ever seen. Unable to stop her, Alina placed herself in front of Red, shoving her hands against her chest.

"Stop! You have to fight it!"

Alina received no response, and was simply pushed through the mud and dirt by Red's preternatural strength. Rocks dug into her flesh, her feet covered in gunk. Looking up in a last-ditch effort to break through to her, Alina nearly collapsed with shock. Red's eyes were fully white, rolled so far back into her head that they appeared upside down.

Alina lost her balance as Red continued to walk. She fell to the ground, hands sinking into the mud. Despite her best efforts, she was unable to get through—all she could do was watch Red as she walked into the Mørke Forest. Like a ghost made of flesh and blood, she floated through the darkness until it consumed her, taking herself into the maw of the Wolf.

Alina scrambled to her feet and ran one last time toward Red. She should have known when she fell in love with Red so easily—the protection spell failed. She had no time to think about the other girls' suffering. Wiping tears from her eyes as she raced into the forest, she tripped over a looping root and hit her chin against the earth.

With a panicked whimper and the taste of blood in her mouth, Alina caught one last glimpse of Red as she disappeared into the trees.

Only when she was completely gone did Alina pick herself up off the ground. Like she, too, was possessed, Alina walked without thought. Not home, where she could hide behind thick doors and bolted locks. Instead, covered in mud and blood, Alina headed to the opposite side of town to the derelict outskirts where newcomers made their homes along the river, where the poorest of Silvania resided.

Where Sorin Nabita lived.

14

OCLEAU

THE YEAR OF THE CURSE

MATTHIAS

The two walked in silence along the crooked path, shrouded with cloaks that sheltered their faces from anyone who passed by. They did not encounter anyone once they met on the edge of town, two days after Ana demanded he use his fists to create the bruises that now marred her skin. Thankful for the chance to remain anonymous and unseen, Matthias and Ana made the long walk to Azalea's home deep in the woods, so far from town that she could practice her Craft with little risk. Though she was safe by default—people needed her skills, though they'd never admit it—she could never be too careful about anything.

Though everyone suspected his mother was a witch, and many sought her abilities for their gain, Azalea always looked out for herself. Herbs and potions were not considered witchcraft to those who needed them. Lifesaving tonics that made horrible illnesses ebb and fade, herbal mixtures that encouraged a healthy pregnancy... When people needed help, they didn't consider it witchcraft, and they were happy enough to take what was offered.

Despite her occasional good deed, her dark magic was always at play. She possessed a strange connection to the forest; even the birds seemed to flock to her. It gave Matthias a chill every time he thought about the way the forest reacted when she was near. Her beastly crow watched out for her, ensuring she and Juniper always remained safe. Yet whenever Matthias tried to accept her, thinking about how things were not all good or all bad, he was reminded that it was her witchcraft that killed Riina, who was guilty of nothing except loving him.

Though dark, Azalea practiced her Craft in a subtle way. A man accused of rape but not charged would be found dead of strange circumstances, his body flopped over his horse-drawn cart, eyes plucked out by ravens and crows. Because of these abilities, Azalea was the only woman for miles who owned land; no one dared take it away from her.

Even with the forest surrounding them, the trees leaning towards them as though they were listening, there was still beauty to be seen. Ahead on the path stood a beautiful doe, nibbling bark along the edge of a tree. It spotted them, its beady black eyes wary, and continued to nibble as it kept an eye on them. They walked past without getting too close, and she went back to eating once they moved beyond her. It proved that, despite the nefarious things that disturbed these woods, there was still a natural order and serenity about them.

"I must remind you, my mother is the most untrusting, evil woman I have ever had the poor luck to know," Matthias said.

"She helps women. She can make women fertile or not if they do not wish to have children—such a thing can mean life or death for someone. I know she has protected women from similar situations before. A woman will always support another woman in a case like this," Ana said confidently.

"But it is *not* a case like that. If she so much as suspects, even for a second, that you are lying..."

"I'll end up drowned in the lake." Ana smiled. "I understand the risk, Matthias."

"I won't let her do anything to you," Matthias promised, then immediately winced when he thought back to two days prior. *Laying a hand on her was wrong.*

Fortunately, Ana seemed to harbor no ill will against him for it and continued to remind him that he did it at her behest. He hadn't slept right since the incident, and it haunted him to know he could hit a woman. Even one who asked him to do it.

The silence that followed seemed to echo with shared emotion; the promise of freedom was fragile, hanging on by a thread that could be severed at any moment. However, neither spoke of the delicate balance as they continued on.

At last, the house crept into sight, black plumes of smoke sputtering from an unclean chimney and souring the air. The two-story house leaned sideways, crooked from years of neglect, tilting to loom toward the east. The surrounding trees leaned over it protectively, their leaves making a nest around the perimeter. Underneath one of the windows was a smudge of coal, reminding Matthias of what Juniper had said about the vandalism. Witch trials were ramping up in other towns; Matthias wondered how long it would be until they reached Ocleau. *Maybe they really do need me to stay.*

Matthias led the way up the warped stairs, each step groaning under their weight. Moments later, the door opened to Juniper surveying her brother and the woman standing beside him.

"Brother, we were not expecting company." Her voice was sweet, with a hint of disappointment. She used her body to shield what was behind her while Azalea shuffled things around in the house.

"It's alright, she knows everything," Matthias replied confidently, masking his irritation and confirming that Ana was with him solely to help free him from his curse. Juniper surely would not think him fool enough to bring a woman here after what Azalea did to Riina. One slip-up could reveal how Matthias felt about her. *How much can I trust her?*

Juniper's eyes narrowed. She gripped Matthias's arm and pulled him into the house. The warm and musty smell of damp wood burning surrounded him. She pulled him close so she could whisper in his ear. "You did this without consulting us?"

"It was an opportunity I could not pass up. She is the answer to our problem." Matthias pulled away from his sister, disturbed by her sudden resemblance to Azalea. She was not the sweet, innocent girl he remembered, but he blamed himself for that. He never gave her the chance to get away from their mother.

"When did you find her? Today?"

"Three days ago." Matthias regretted the words immediately.

"Three days is plenty of time to warn us." Juniper eyed him with a touch of frustration, then sighed, her shoulders dropping.

Juniper walked to the open door, where Ana stood awkwardly. "My apologies, we are simply caught off guard," she explained, welcoming her in.

"Then you have my sincerest apologies for impeding your day," Ana replied quaintly. "My name is Ana."

"I am Juniper, Matthias's sister." Juniper brought Ana in by the crook of her elbow. She shut the door behind them to prevent more cold air from blowing in. "Come, warm yourself by the fire. May I take your cloak?"

Ana carefully removed her cloak, her movements stiff with pain, revealing her facial bruises. Juniper noticed but kept her expression neutral. Matthias knew it was something she saw frequently. So many abused women came through the house, begging for something to kill their husbands or something to at least numb the pain.

Azalea stepped into the living room then, studying Ana suspiciously. Matthias hoped she didn't see the resemblance between Ana and Riina, that it had been long enough that the memory had faded. That Ana's brown hair was contrast enough from Riina's blonde.

Juniper stepped out of the way to hang Ana's cloak up, and Azalea swooped in like a vulture.

"Your son told me about the curse he has, a dreadful, fearful thing," Ana began. Her voice wavered slightly. "My husband craves power and will see this curse as such. As much as I do not wish for him to have more power... It is my hope he will be caught and tried swiftly. He will want it but needs the incentive to seek you out."

"What do you propose?" Azalea asked.

"To appear ill enough that simple methods will not help, only the cures from a healer. He will come to you—"

"Why would he want to save the woman he beats?" Azalea asked sharply.

Ana lowered her head, shifting so that her sleeves inched upwards. It was subtle enough that any onlooker would see it as unintentional, but Matthias knew it was to show the bruises around her wrists. Tears fell from Ana's eyes, dropping at her feet to stain the wood. She wiped them away furiously, then met Azalea's gaze.

"He begs my forgiveness every time, tells me how *sorry* he is," Ana told her weakly. "I...I used to believe him. But it never ends."

Matthias felt her words as they cut into him like daggers, branding him with guilt even though he knew this was her plan. He distracted himself by watching the fire in an attempt to keep Azalea from sensing his guilt.

"And you wish for him to have more power?" Azalea inquired suspiciously.

"I wish for a reason to leave Ocleau. I have a friend who will help get me out of the town, perhaps out of the country. I've heard Silvania is nice." Ana sighed. "I cannot leave my husband without a viable excuse. Once he has sabotaged the town's trust in him, once he is a monster, they will let me leave him. At the very least, he will not pursue me should I flee. I trust the authorities to catch him; they will be too occupied to worry about me leaving."

Azalea considered her words for a moment, then appeared to accept them. Turning her back to them, she went to the table covered in books and scrolls. Fingers deftly flipped through until she found the book she wanted. She carried it spread open on her forearm. Instead of going to Ana, she went straight to Juniper, who began reading and making small noises of agreement.

"We will do this for you," Azalea said to Ana. "Under one condition."

Ana waited.

"We need protection. If we go through with this, a young and inexperienced werewolf will be roaming free and hungry. They go after the ones they love in familiar places. You will be forced to flee the moment we make this change. Do you understand?" Azalea continued without waiting for Ana's response. "We will likely be the next target, so I must make safeguards."

"Understandable," Ana said softly.

"If we do this for you, we get to control him."

15

SILVANIA

THE YEAR OF THE MOON

SORIN

A pattering noise startled Sorin from sleep, but she woke with instant alertness. She sat up in bed and turned towards the noise. Her window glowed bright white. At first, she thought it was a vivid dream, but when her eyes adjusted, she saw Alina's face pressed against the glass, each heavy breath coating the window in fog. Frantic fingertips rattled against the surface in a desperate way.

Sorin hurried to her feet, her night dress clinging to her body as she made it to the window. With a shove of her shoulder, she managed to force the window open, wincing slightly from the pain.

"What is wrong?" Sorin asked quietly but sternly.

"It's Red," Alina told her, out of breath. Tears had left streaks down her face, and dirt had caked on her nightgown.

Sorin didn't need to know more—Alina's panicked state was enough. She grabbed her black cloak and slung it over her shoulders, feeling the warmth of the material as its weight pulled it down. She slipped on her shoes and climbed out the window, quietly cursing as she smacked her elbow into the sash.

Sorin grabbed Alina's arm and led her away until they were safe from prying eyes. "Tell me everything."

Alina took a deep breath, trying desperately to compose herself. It was a talent she mastered from a young age, keeping her head on straight or at least appearing that way to others. It protected her from gaining unwanted attention. Sorin could see right through it and knew immediately that Alina had not been protected from love; the spell had somehow failed. She'd fallen in love with Red. "I saw her walking through the streets. Something was controlling her, Sorin." Alina calmed herself down enough to speak without hiccups. "I yelled, I pushed her back...no matter what I did, she wouldn't stop."

"Your spell to prevent love must not have worked," Sorin mused. "When you both joined blood during Red's initiation, it may have created conflict in the magic."

"We have to save her," Alina begged.

It became clear to Sorin that the protection spell—at least for Red—had not worked either. Alina was hopelessly in love with Red, and Red was sacrificed to the Wolf.

Sorin pressed her lips into a tight line, looking at Alina. The weight of saving Red was on her shoulders now, and it was a heavy burden to bear. Pressing her fingers to her temples to relieve her building stress, Sorin wondered if it was possible to break the dreaded curse. Though she knew little about it, having only moved to the town recently, she knew it was not a typical sacrifice. There was only one fact that every version of the story agreed upon—a seasoned witch created the curse. It would take a seasoned witch to break it.

No answers came, and Sorin grew frustrated when her train of thought ran nowhere. There was no answer dangling in front of her, not even just out of reach. There was nothing. She looked at Alina, realizing she wouldn't accept that as a response. Instead, she kept quiet.

"We could go after her," Alina suggested. "Perhaps she was protected from the Wolf but not the curse; maybe he won't be able to lay a hand on her."

"You really believe the Wolf molests them?" Sorin asked, her thick brow arched. Her words hung in the air, making Alina frown.

"That's what all the stories say." Alina sounded so young when she said it.

"My parents never read me the story," Sorin said. Her parents never knew of Silvania, the Wolf that haunted it, or the witchcraft that it held. "I have heard bits and pieces. The story of a wolf who will take any woman who has been defiled and steal them away? I know that many, many girls in this town have been *defiled* and are still safe and sound. Alina, it is just a story adults use to keep their girls obedient. They have always wanted to keep women subservient; everywhere I have lived has been the same. Perhaps this Wolf is not as cruel as he is made out to be. The legend states a daughter is to be sacrificed to the Wolf, then he will slaughter a bloodline of the initiator's choosing."

Young women came to Sorin's home in a desperate attempt to prevent pregnancy after a night of bliss. She had seen many faces, and they still wandered Silvania without consequences because Sorin ensured it. Already, she had drawn too much attention to herself and her abilities. Shamed for being different and a newcomer who struggled to learn the language in her first few months there, being a known witch only made things worse. Knowing the protection spell was failing, Sorin wondered how much longer she could remain in Silvania before they ran her out of town.

Alina sighed, bringing Sorin back to the present, to what was relevant now. "But he has *her*." A crease formed between Alina's brows as tears threatened again.

Sorin pursed her lips, then dipped her head into a single nod. "He does. So we go find her."

Alina looked relieved, then worried. "What will we do? Ask for her back?"

Sorin frowned, wishing Alina would stop asking questions she didn't have the answers to. Going in without anything more than her next step was Sorin's plan. She grabbed her shoulders. Though she did not believe her own words, she told Alina what she needed to hear. "The protection spell may hold, and that is all we have to work with. We must work with it for Red's sake."

Alina nodded. "You are right. We must try."

Sorin released Alina and looked in the direction of the forest. A forest she spent so much time in and fell in love with, the only safe place she could retreat into. A place where energy surrounded and caressed her, never threatening to uproot her. While many felt safe within the town's borders, Sorin always felt the eyes of scrutiny on her. As if someone waited for her to slip up, to reveal her true nature and her Craft. In the forest, she felt safe. But now, as she peered into the dark woods, she felt afraid for the first time.

She put on a brave face for Alina and grabbed her hand. "Come, we cannot waste any more time."

They soon reached Alina's house, where she had last seen Red as she cut through in her possessed state, bracing themselves for what they might find. Before they made it into the woods, a shrill scream filled the air from two houses down.

16

OCLEAU

THE YEAR OF THE CURSE

MATTHIAS

Matthias watched Azalea's face carefully as she waited for Ana's reply. From her stony expression, he could tell it was a test to see if Ana was being truthful about her husband. If he truly beat her, she would not be opposed to him being abused in return. A wolf controlled by a witch had been attempted many times before. In trials all around the continent, men and women were caught after a full moon frenzy, and they pointed their bloodied fingers at a witch—often an innocent woman—who was strung up alongside them for her crimes. Azalea did not wish to draw more attention to herself and her family, but the protection of a wolf proved to be quite tempting.

Ana stammered, "C-control him?"

"It may not be possible," Azalea explained, bitterness filling her voice. "But should I find the correct spell, I will protect my family using your husband. A werewolf in town is dangerous and unpredictable; they kill and they create packs. My family could be the first he slaughters because he smells that his wife has been here. I can make sure it is not *you* who he comes for."

Ana winced at the words, visibly stung.

"Azalea, do not be cruel," Matthias countered.

"The world is cruel, Matthias; it is time you learned that."

Matthias glared at his mother. "I learned firsthand from you."

Ana shifted from foot to foot, her discomfort nearly palpable. "You may have him," she said. "If you think it will protect this town and your family, I have no reason to deny you this."

Azalea grinned. "Very well. Take a seat. Juniper and I will brew up something to make you ill."

"Appear ill," Matthias corrected.

"Appearing ill and being ill is no different." Azalea sneered. "The only difference is what I create will not inevitably kill her."

Ana sat as she was told. She was putting herself in the hands of Azalea and Juniper, and Matthias was trusting that they would give her something to appear ill. Trusting that it wouldn't kill her. So much was at stake, dangling on a delicate thread—one wrong move and it would snap.

Matthias knew how quickly Azalea would kill Ana if she thought there was anything between them. Even though he wasn't even sure if there was anything between them at all. *A connection, yes, but does she feel it too?* She gave nothing away. He debated the idea that he was forcing her into a role she never asked for; he had more he could offer her, but it was not the time to bring it up. They needed to build a stronger bond first.

Matthias realized he was staring at Ana and quickly glanced away. He turned his attention to Azalea and Juniper, who were muttering over the cluttered table. The gentle clinking of clay mortar and pestles rang through the house, echoed by the crackle of the fire and the murmurs of the two witches as they worked at their altar. To keep himself busy, Matthias went to the fire and pushed back the charred logs to place a fresh one on. Knowing that Azalea and Juniper were distracted, he offered a warm glance to Ana to calm her nerves.

A hibernating spider scurried out from the warmth of the log—a shelter for bugs and rodents all throughout the year—and frantically looked for an escape. It scuttled from one end of the log to the other, but the fire wrapped hot fingers along the edges, trapping it and closing in on it second by second. Matthias reached in to save it—he had seen enough death in his life—but it succumbed to the flame before he could get the chance.

"Excuse me, brother." Juniper spoke softly as she walked over to him, too quietly for him to notice right away.

He stepped aside, his eyes still locked in on the spot where the spider had once been. Juniper interrupted his line of sight, her simple black skirt pooling around her like a tent. With deft hands, she poured the contents of a clay bowl into the iron one hanging from the fireplace.

While it brewed at a rolling boil, Azalea passed Juniper a wooden board with a small blade and other tools upon it. Matthias watched his mother walk back to the table and reach underneath. She grunted as she hoisted out a jar full of wiggling black creatures. She plucked one out and brought it over to Juniper, who withdrew from her pocket a rat. Its tail curled around her wrist.

Matthias shuddered.

Juniper smiled playfully. "Shall I fetch you a bucket?"

Matthias ignored the sick feeling in his stomach, saying nothing. He checked on Ana, who remained seated, watching closely. *How can all three women not be squeamish of those foul creatures?* he wondered.

Juniper set the rat down on the wooden board, stroking its fur. Then she took the leech from Azalea and placed it on the rat. As it latched on, the rodent protested with shrieks that faded out into heavy panting as Juniper whispered words so soft and quiet Matthias couldn't understand them. After a few moments, she plucked the leech from the rat, which scurried up the front of her dress and nestled in her hair.

As though the Craft took over Juniper's body, she moved with a grace unnatural to the horrific actions she was performing. With two sharp pins, she poked them through either side of the leech, holding it there. Using the blade, she slit along its underside. Black and red oozed out of it. Juniper cut out two sections, carefully removing them and placing them in the iron pot. The rat climbed back down from her shoulder to smell the dissected leech.

Matthias had to look away as it ravenously consumed the pieces. Instead, he watched Juniper ladle the brew into a funnel and strain the solids into a phial. Murky in color, it reminded Matthias of the night sky without stars, an endless sort of darkness. Like death. It smelled rancid like carrion left out in the sun too long. Juniper capped the phial with a cork stopper and gave it a shake.

Azalea swooped in and snatched it from Juniper's hands; she released it as though they had rehearsed, their movements flawlessly choreographed. As Azalea closed in on Ana, Matthias stiffened. The woman grabbed Ana's hands and lifted them, studying the marks around her wrists. Then her eyes danced along to her eye and cheek, which was swollen and red, with purplish green bruising around the edges.

Matthias refused to look away in fear they would see through him. Juniper, whose eyes studied him thoroughly, would see his guilt at being the one who created the bruises if he looked away. *Ana must have added the ones on her cheek and eye after I left,* he thought, *knowing I couldn't take it that far.*

"These are fresh. Is your husband home?" Azalea asked, her grip tightening on Ana's chin.

It was as if Ana was the witch on trial. One wrong movement and she would be hanged or tied to the pyre to be burned alive. Azalea's methods of killing were subtler, more insidious, certainly more dangerous. Matthias eyed the phial nervously.

Ana shook her head. "He left on his final hunt of the season."

"When will he return? It must be before the full moon. That is scarcely a fortnight away."

"He has never been gone longer than a week," Ana told her. "He will be home in three days, at the latest."

Azalea reached out to hand the phial to Ana but snatched it back. She clutched it to her breast, her knuckles growing white as she held onto it. A cruel look crossed her face.

"Drink it now," Azalea demanded. "Then I will know you're not using this to turn me in, using my son to get the proof you need for this town to finally have me burned."

"Azalea!" Matthias shouted, stepping in between her and Ana.

Azalea smacked Matthias with the back of her hand.

His cheek burned from the impact, but he hardly jerked back at the assault. "The full moon is two weeks from now—she should not suffer from being ill for so long. Let her take it a week from now. What good would it do her to out you? Everyone in town knows what you are."

"I don't trust her," Azalea replied.

"And I do not trust you."

"I will take it," Ana said passively, trying to calm the storm around her. "If I fall ill while he is away, it will be more believable. The chance of him stumbling onto the potion and discovering what I am up to before I have the chance to leave... It may be enough for him to kill me."

"She is right," Juniper added.

Matthias shrunk back, defeated.

"The moment her husband returns, you will give her something to heal her," Matthias demanded.

"Very well," Azalea agreed and handed the phial to Ana at last.

Ana stared at the molasses-like substance inside, then uncapped it, looking around for a place to put the cork stopper.

Juniper's hand appeared to take it from her, then handed her a cup of water.

Ana paused, holding the phial in one hand and the cup in the other. Beads of nervous sweat appeared on her forehead as she studied the brew. She took back the potion in one swift swig, following it with the warm water. Her face immediately went white, and the phial clattered to the floor. She swooned, toppling from the chair and crumpling onto the floor beside the chair, black froth at her mouth.

Matthias's head spun.

"What have you done?"

17

SILVANIA

THE YEAR OF THE MOON

RED

Though Red could not see, she felt everything. Being conscious without control of her own body proved to be the most terrifying experience of her life. More than facing her grandmother, more than being locked in a closet for days. The moment the curse slammed into her chest; she knew it had begun: the long walk to her death.

As the thing controlling her body made its way to the forest, she felt someone trying to stop her. She heard the distant echo of a familiar voice, one that warmed her inside. But nothing stopped her, not hands being shoved against her collarbone, not the desperate plea of someone she couldn't quite place.

Red barrelled through any obstacle that appeared before her and though she could not see, she sensed the overbearing presence of the woods as she crossed the town line. Its power latched onto her, wisps curling around her body to embrace her. The sweet smell of moisture in the air was fresh and light, a contrast to the curse that had its grip on her. Silence fell over her the moment she stepped beyond the town line; it felt like peace for a few seconds. Suddenly, her eyes rolled out of their unnatural position and adjusted to the darkness surrounding her. It was as though the possession ended as soon as she entered the

Wolf's territory. A gust of wind went right through her, and she gasped, collapsing to the forest floor. Her hands clutched the cold dirt between her fingers, trying to absorb the power of nature like Sorin or Alina were able to do.

Alina.

She tried to stop me.

Red stood, and dizziness consumed her. She stumbled, gripping a tree to keep herself from toppling over. When her vertigo passed, she took a quick look around the forest to confirm she was not going to be attacked, then looked back over the town line. A border appeared between the forest and the town, subtly blocking her path like the heatwave given off by a fire stared at too long.

Fighting the eerie pull of the forest, Red approached the border. She touched it but found she could not penetrate it. She swallowed nervously, trying to gather her wits. *I cannot go back.*

She knew what came next: the Wolf.

Furious at the realization that the protection spell did not work, Red wondered what could be done to change her situation. She refused to accept death.

Staring down the crooked path that led to her grandmother's house, Red decided she would hole up there. The Wolf would come for her there, and she smirked at the thought of shoving her grandmother in the way of its maw, watching the sharp teeth rip apart her wrinkled, papery flesh.

Even if the Wolf came for her next, she would have a brief moment of peace.

Satisfied with her plan, Red began the journey to her grandmother's without looking back. Fog swept in, creeping up from the tree roots like the hands of a hundred ghosts, extending higher and higher so nothing could be seen, not even Red's bright hood.

Step by step, she navigated the unruly terrain, grasping the trees for help. Through the fog that clouded her mind, she wondered if the Mørke forest, alive with its untethered power, was truly moving. A large root shifted as she stepped over, catching onto the toe of her boot and knocking her down.

Red hit the ground. She could smell the fertile soil as she disrupted it with her impact. Frustrated, she shouted at the Earth, "You're supposed to give me power!"

The forest stopped moving, obeying her command and ceasing its trickery.

Red composed herself and got back to her feet. Where the dirt covered her, the skin tingled like a healing wound. She took a few deep breaths, trying to separate reality from fiction, and continued on.

Suddenly, Red felt a pair of eyes on her, forcing her to stop. As it had before, her conscious body functions ceased. Red froze like prey in the eyes of a predator, hoping she would remain unnoticed. Darting off would not only get her lost, but it was also certain to get her killed.

Think about how brave your friends are, Red thought. *Tatiana and Lilianna face their beast of a father each night, Sorin looks over her shoulder, wondering when the townsfolk will decide to drive her out...or, worse, light her pyre. And Alina, the sort of love she feels is unnatural to the small-minded.*

The pair of eyes appeared in the fog, soot-black and glimmering as though lit from within. Instead of cowering or begging for her life like she might have done a few days ago, Red stared back and waited to see what they belonged to. A wolf? Or a man?

When a stick broke, Red knew it was a man; animals were not that careless. At first, Red was comforted by the thought, but an insidious feeling crept in. Throughout her life, she had never been harmed by an animal...but had been struck many times by a man. *Men are more dangerous than wolves.*

"W-who's there?" The words came out chalky, her voice crackling.

At last, he stepped into view—a tall man with scraggly brown hair, unkempt like he had never run a comb through it in his life. He would have been comely had his eyes not been such a deep black, like the night without stars. Red felt their intense gaze reading every single part of her. He was shirtless, his burly torso riddled with ancient scars, and his trousers were filthy, covered in the patchwork of a man who didn't know how to sew.

He stared blankly at her, his lips slightly parted as though he wanted to speak but couldn't form the words.

Red couldn't help but wonder if the man before her had lived so long in the woods that he lost his humanity—or if he even had it in the first place. The little she knew of the Wolf came from the legends told to her as a child—stories of a dangerous wolf-man lurking in these woods, waiting for the sacrifice of a daughter so he could defile her. *I'm not about to let this scraggly forest-dwelling man touch me.* She did not feel threatened by him as he stood there, not making any move to get closer to her.

"Who are you?" she asked more directly.

His eyes darted up to meet hers, a sudden look of defeat on his face. His lips remained parted, and she saw his tongue move to form words, but only a sort of breath came out, betraying his frustration and shame. Exhaustion hollowed out his features as if he'd been defeated by the curse. For the first time, Red felt an odd sense of sympathy for such a creature.

Father must have wanted Mayor Fischer dead, she thought, remembering his rants toward the Mayor and his family. It was clear that her father coveted the office of Mayor. A chill ran down her spine. The mayor's son, Sebastian, was near her age, and his daughter, Celeste, was six. But it was her life that mattered now.

Red studied him. This was—he was—like nothing she expected. "Y-you are the Wolf?" she asked.

He seemed to register something with her words, and he slowly nodded.

"Have you come to kill me?" *Maybe this should have been my first question.*

She took a step forward, struck by the powerful instinct to become the bigger predator, to be the braver one. After all, the Wolf she was so afraid of turned out to be mute, scraggly, and almost frightened of her presence in his forest. She recalled tales of a witch creating him. Red had the power of the craft within her; perhaps he sensed it.

His eyes narrowed as she approached, taking in her face in the dim light. Something made him flinch; his eyes widened, and he took a step back as if preparing to run from her.

I am nothing to fear, she thought as curiosity ate away her terror. Devoured it whole, and she was no longer afraid. The roles reversed, predator now fearing prey, Red had the power now. *Or maybe I am the power.*

He let out a shaky breath, then slowly answered her with a shake of his head.

No, he was not there to kill her.

18

OCLEAU

THE YEAR OF THE CURSE

AZALEA

Azalea watched Ana crumple to the floor, convulsing and frothing at the mouth. Matthias knelt before her, placing a firm hand on her shoulder and tilting her sideways to thrust a finger into her mouth so she could breathe more easily.

A memory from when Matthias was but a child flooded Azalea. Only it was Matthias's father who was convulsing on the ground, face bloated, breaths turning into empty gasps. *I tried so hard to keep him alive*, Azalea thought. She looked at how tenderly Matthias was coaxing Ana to breathe. *He is so much like his father*.

A few moments passed, and the color came back to Ana's cheeks. Her breathing returned to normal, and her eyes began to focus. They locked with Matthias's, and her expression softened.

"Ana?" Matthias asked gently, though a subtle hint of anger still lingered in his voice.

She tried to speak but succumbed to a coughing fit. She used his sturdy body to pull herself upright into a sitting position. Matthias helped her to her feet, but Ana was hardly able to stand without clinging to him. Staring vacantly at the floor, she wavered while Matthias steadied her.

Juniper filled a cup of water and brought it to Ana, helping her take a sip. Most of it spilled down her chin, so Juniper stepped back, dipping her head down so the water splashed onto the floor.

Matthias glared at his mother, but she spoke first.

"This is good. She has proven herself strong enough to handle what I have given her—she'll make it. You do not need to worry about her surviving now, Matthias." She grinned. "Unless, of course, her husband does not arrive or does not willingly take your curse; then, it will most certainly kill her in two weeks' time... Or you will."

"How can you sleep at night? Do you not harbor an ounce of guilt for the innocent lives you take? The lives you hold in your grasp, just tight enough so they do not slip, yet you can crush them at a moment's urge?"

"It is because of my grasp on everything around me that I do sleep at night," she spat. She gestured towards the door. "Go on now. Get her out of my sight."

Matthias yanked Ana's cloak from the peg near the door and jerked the door open with such ferocity, Azalea was surprised it didn't come off the ancient hinges. With a slam, Matthias was gone.

Smiling, she walked to the window and opened it, finding herself face-to-face with her trustworthy familiar, Aegidius. She stroked the crow's soft black feathers, feeling the smoothness that allowed him to glide through the air, cutting through the fiercest of winds to get where she needed him to be.

"My sweet," she crooned. "Follow them at a distance, and keep a close eye on Matthias."

With a soft kiss between his black eyes, Azalea sent him off. Listening was more valuable than coin, gold, or jewels. Secrets haunted every town, every family. They held so much power over others if one knew of them. Often Azalea chose to be paid in secrets instead of coin. Coin could purchase necessities and luxuries, but secrets could keep her and Juniper alive. Now that Matthias was back in Ocleau, they would keep him alive, too.

"Juniper." Azalea beckoned her daughter.

She guided her to a kitchen table covered in all manner of scripts, scrolls, and books full of spells and incantations; there would be something in there that they could use to control the Wolf.

Azalea spread her hands over the documents. "We have work to do."

They began without delay, pouring hours of their time into reading every line twice to decipher any hidden meanings or riddles within the spells, pondering the best way to control a person. There were temporary possessions; Azalea had dabbled in possession more than once, but to be in the body of the Wolf was not her intention. *I need full control of the beast to command it at my will. Not simply a werewolf I can leash, a wolf that can change at my whim. A wolf that will come to my every beck and call.*

It sounded impossible, but Azalea had long learned that the impossible only remained so until a witch found a way to create what she needed.

"Mama." Juniper walked into the room with two mugs of tea. She gracefully handed one to Azalea.

Azalea looked at her curiously.

"Something is not right about this," Juniper admitted.

"If you do not agree with what I want to do, you do not have to be a part of it," Azalea told her. She knew her daughter's moral code was very different from her own, but Azalea had always sheltered and protected her so she wouldn't turn out as viciously cynical as herself. Every time Azalea looked at Juniper, she recalled the betrayal and hurt but found she could still love her daughter.

Juniper shook her head. "Not the wolf." She set down the steaming mug, leaving her fingers faintly red from the heat. With the soft expression on her round face and her button nose, she still looked so young and innocent to Azalea. She wondered if a time would come when this would change. *Maybe I've protected her too much.*

Juniper snapped Azalea out of her thoughts. "I mean Ana. There is something about her that I do not trust."

"She looks so much like Riina," Azalea said. She noticed immediately when Ana walked into the house. The similarities between the two were uncanny. While Azalea had more up her sleeve than Matthias or Juniper ever knew, it was obvious Matthias also had a plan. Confident she would figure out his ploy first, she wasn't worried. *I love my son, but he is no mastermind.*

"Yes," Juniper agreed. "Matthias is a very loving person. It would not surprise me if he fell in love with a woman who looks like Riina. Perhaps he has already fallen in love with her and is trying to get her husband out of the way."

Azalea pondered this, unable to deny that the thought had occurred to her too. "He has too much at stake. If he loves her, he knows how easily I can make her drown herself, hang herself, poison herself. If he does love her, he would do best to stay away from her. He belongs to this family, and I will not have him trying to leave us again for another pretty face. Love is for family, not harlots."

Juniper nodded, though she looked pensive. "Why do you want to keep him so badly?"

Azalea's lips tightened, and creases formed at her eyes. "Before you were conceived, I loved someone very much. With that man, I had Matthias, and when he was dying, I did everything in my power to save him. It wasn't enough. Matthias is all I have left of him."

Juniper dropped her head, knowing her conception was very different. However, she made no more comments about Matthias and his father. "But Mama, how will you keep him here?"

"Simple, child." Azalea grinned. "When it is all over, we will kill Ana, and he will have no one left in this world but us."

"That is what drove him away last time," Juniper warned.

"We will have a wolf in our command, a guard dog to protect us. If the displacement should fail with Ana's husband, then Matthias will be the one we control. Either way, I will have a wolf, whether it be

Matthias or Ana's husband." Azalea kept her eyes locked on her young daughter, waiting for her reaction. Would she agree with keeping her older brother around to protect them when the hellions came?

But Juniper's expression revealed nothing, and she went back to work without another word.

19

SILVANIA

THE YEAR OF THE MOON

RED

They were at an impasse. Red knew she couldn't return to the town or her home. She knew this man before her did not want to harm her like she originally thought, but she was left dangling with her questions unanswered. The cold crept in around them as though it had forgotten until now. The darkness of the forest seemed even thicker than before, and Red yearned to be somewhere safe.

But nowhere was safe for her anymore.

"Do you have a name?" Red asked him, hoping humanity would thaw his frozen tongue.

He cocked his head to the side with a questioning look, making it clear he did not know it. Or perhaps he could not remember it after all these years. If Red recalled the stories correctly, the last time the Wolf had been summoned to kill a bloodline was over two hundred years ago.

Red had gone days without speaking, locked in her room, and fed meals twice a day; even in that short amount of time, the first words that came out of her mouth felt wrong. Without anyone around her, there was no need to talk. She understood the difficulty he experienced after hundreds of years.

"Alright, if you aren't going to speak… Can you speak?" She changed direction.

He nodded slowly, his expression pinched as though he wasn't certain of his answer. At the very least, he understood her. *I can work with that,* she thought.

"Is there somewhere warm we can go? It is the middle of the night and it is freezing," she said.

I'm telling the Wolf what to do, she thought. She was unsure where her confidence came from, but she embraced it, nonetheless. Was it the powers of the earth, or was it her growing realization that she had the upper hand in this situation? She'd never held power before; the feeling tantalized her senses.

He glanced over his shoulder, then looked back at her and gestured with a head jerk. He turned and walked back through the fog he arrived in. Red quickly followed. His bare feet padded silently over the detritus lining the forest floor, his agile legs preventing him from tripping over the roots that reached up to grab at Red's ankles. It seemed as though he owned this forest; it bowed down and made way for him.

They continued through the woods, far from the path Red had followed her entire life. Fear gripped her, a ghost of a hand that clamped around her throat, letting her struggle until the grip was so tight, she could no longer breathe. *There are forces at play much darker than what the coven plays with*, she thought. To calm herself, she took deep, even breaths.

Red followed the very man who was supposed to kill her, wondering if the daughters sacrificed before her never faced the horrible ends promised to them. She wondered what really happened to the girls in all the bedtime stories. *What if parents just filled in the blanks to curb undesired behavior?* she thought.

In the distance, a cabin appeared. Dead vines wrapped their skeleton bodies along the sides, snaking up around the roof, pulling the thatch away in places. Moss grew between the logs that made up the walls. Small and modest, the smell of rotting wood and old soot wafted out the moment he opened the door. Red felt the ancient energy inside, waiting to get out. It breathed them in as they entered. He crossed the threshold first, moving across creaking wood planks. She followed tentatively, eyeing the dusty cobwebs dancing in the corners. It was colder in the house than outside, but the Wolf quickly went to build a fire.

Red studied her surroundings, looking for a second exit, though she didn't plan on running. The cabin was made entirely of smooth, well-crafted logs despite the vegetation that took over the exterior, giving it the appearance of nature reclaiming it. The small living area contained a fireplace and a few pieces of scarred wooden furniture, including a table that dominated the space. There was one other door that she guessed led to a bedroom. Otherwise, the place seemed abandoned.

She looked down at her hands, white from the cold, and watched color return to them as the fire grew. Red turned to face the man, clearing her throat to get his attention. It was time to take her life into her own hands once and for all.

He stood in the corner of the cabin, watching her curiously. A shadow danced along his figure, but his eyes still glowed with the flame.

"I don't believe you mean to hurt me. Nor that you wish to, nor that you are meant to. Is this true?" she asked.

He looked up at her with a sideways glance, then nodded. His lips opened to speak and for the first time, he managed words. Words that sounded like he had a mouthful of gravel. "S...safe."

"I am safe? With you?"

He shook his head, scowling at his inability to speak freely. His mouth opened, then clamped shut. A growl emitted from his throat, full of anger at his failings. His shoulders sunk down, and he exhaled a long breath before trying again. "You...sacri...ficed."

"By my father, yes," Red said bitterly.

"Broken." His guttural words made Red cringe.

"The curse?" she asked, stepping forward quickly enough to make the man flinch further back into the corner. "It worked..." she mumbled to herself, thinking of the protection spell. Then she looked up at the man. "What do I call you?"

Once again, the man had no answer for her, and Red had to accept that he was either ashamed of it or he could no longer remember. She pursed her lips together while an idea brewed in her mind; if the curse had been enacted, but failed because she was protected from the Wolf, then perhaps the Wolf would protect her in return.

Thoughts bubbled up, unable to be held down from years of abuse. When she was five and scolded for tracking dirt into the house. When she was seven and slept too long. When she was eight, for dropping a basket of eggs. When she was fourteen, and began to blossom.

I have an opportunity to take control of my life.

"You show no sign of ill intent, no desire to harm me." Red voiced her observations. "You've brought me here, given me shelter and warmth, and protected me from being out in the forest overnight; the cold would certainly have killed me. I have a proposition."

His black eyes narrowed, crow's feet appearing in the corners. His eyebrows pulled down into slants, not angry, but curious. Disappointment darkened his expression at the thought of another person using him for what he was.

Before guilt or fear could control her, she told him the truth. "I need you to help me."

He said nothing but met her eyes.

"I need you to protect me from the ones who sacrificed me. I need you to kill my grandmother and my father."

20

OCLEAU

THE YEAR OF THE CURSE

JUNIPER

Dew drops lined the dying grass. With the cold coming, there was scarcely anything left alive, but the forest still thrummed with ancient power. Juniper heaved the bag of flour into the corner of the cellar and covered it with a moth-eaten blanket. Wiping the sweat from her brow, she smiled, sensing the critters hiding out down there for the winter.

"Now, don't indulge too much," she said to them.

The mice and other small animals' eyes were iridescent in the faint light coming from above as they peeked out from their hiding spots. Juniper left the cellar and breathed in the fresh air. Sensing her familiar in the woods, she quietly shut the cellar door and approached the unnamed doe.

"You look well," she said to the animal as she approached. She stroked the coarse hair and felt it prickle her palm. A divot in the doe's neck never grew hair back and was smooth like a river stone. Juniper had found the deer as a fawn, near death with a gash on her neck. She had swaddled the fawn in her coat, brought it home, and nursed it back to health.

Juniper smiled fondly at the memory. *You have work to do,* she told herself.

The doe, not needed by her witch, dipped her head and gently loped back into the expanse of trees.

Juniper looked at the house where she was raised, thinking about her brother inside. He returned cold and closed off after he had brought Ana home. What felt like hours ago was days now; a sense of distrust disrupted the comfort she and her mother had when it was just the two of them. Juniper was surprised Matthias came home after seeing Ana in such a tumultuous state. *But he did come back, just like Mama said,* Juniper thought. *Because he was forced to.* A selfish part of her wanted her brother to stay, but the part of her that loved him knew he was better off leaving.

She took a deep breath to steady herself before entering the house. She tended to the food for the week while she thought about how to get her mother out for a few hours. *I must speak with Matthias alone,* she thought.

"Mama," Juniper called from the kitchen. Her face was red and slicked with sweat from working in such close proximity to heat. Her wrists bore burn marks from misjudging the distance between the hot flames and the pot she cooked in. "Mama!"

Azalea's voice arrived before she did. "Yes, child?"

"We have run low on flour, yeast, spices—how have our stocks run so low this early into the season?" Juniper spotted the look in Azalea's eye. *She knows,* Juniper thought. *She knows I want Matthias alone.*

Azalea rolled her eyes back as though to glance at Matthias's room, where he was still asleep. She did not respond but crossed the kitchen. She opened the cupboard and frowned when she confirmed their stocks were running low. With a furrowed brow, she looked at Juniper and commanded, "You must go into town to get more before the town itself runs dry."

"No, Mama, I have my hands full here," Juniper pleaded. "Could you do it just this once, please?"

Azalea glowered. She rarely left the house unless absolutely necessary. "I will get your brother to do it."

"Oh, Mama, you know how he always gets the wrong things," Juniper persisted. "I ask him for dried sage, he brings me rosemary. He will not get what we need, and then I will have to fetch what he missed. It becomes a waste of time and coin, both of which we are short on."

Azalea's expression was pinched, but Juniper could see she was about to agree.

Juniper had a way about her, an aura that made everyone adore her. She knew she could have anyone wrapped around her finger. But she was too soft, too modest to con others into doing things for her. A hardworking girl who did what she needed to survive the day, Juniper prided herself in her ability to make people trust her—and she was a trustworthy person in most cases.

"Very well." Azalea sighed. "Wake up that brother of yours, though. He cannot sleep in this house and eat our food without contributing."

"More firewood?" Juniper asked, pleased that she would be alone with Matthias for at least the next hour.

"And get him to fix the back door," Azalea added as she grabbed her cloak and opened the front door.

Alone at last, Juniper took a deep breath of relief. Thankfully, her mother forgot about the extra storage under her feet, where Juniper had hidden the extra flour. In a few days' time, she would feign its discovery, blame herself for misplacing it, and laugh at her youthful absentmindedness. She wiped her sweaty hands on her skirt, then hiked it up as she walked up the stairs to wake Matthias. By the time she finished stomping her way there, Matthias opened the door and faced her head-on.

Still exhausted from jagged rest—Juniper often heard him speaking in his sleep and his cries from the frightful nightmares that woke him—he wore only his nightclothes, his hair a matted mess.

Juniper fondly recalled how he struggled to keep it from becoming an unruly mop as a child. Their mother had always kept it short to prevent tangles.

Juniper cleared her throat. "Good morning, Matthias."

"And to you," Matthias replied cautiously. "What are you doing at my door?"

"I need to speak to you about something. Come." She beckoned for him to come downstairs. She moved swiftly, the house a part of her; she could navigate it blind. Matthias stomped heavily behind her.

In the kitchen, Juniper filled two bowls with oats, prepared two mugs of tea, and put out a loaf of day-old bread for them to nibble. A jar in the center of the table held fresh-made butter, one of the things Matthias splurged on when he went to the market.

After learning what their mother planned if the displacement failed, Juniper knew she needed to warn her brother. She wanted to give him the opportunity to make the right choice. Only having just gotten him back, it pained her that the information she would give him now might drive him away, but his safety was her concern. He had the right to make his own choice. *Part of me hopes he will leave now and take the curse with him, as much as it will hurt.* Azalea did not think him capable of living with the moon curse, but she knew people could adapt to anything.

She could stall no longer. "I must begin by stating that, in most situations, I will always side with Mama. However, watching you leave when I was a child and not understanding why my older brother and protector was abandoning me... It broke my heart. I will not lose you again, Matthias, because I love you." Juniper spun her mug around and around in her hands. "I fear that Mama is going to do it again, only this time with Ana."

"Ana?" Matthias's eyebrow shot up. "But I do not even know the woman—she is not... No one can replace Riina."

"We are not blind, we are women," Juniper said wryly. "I want Ana to be safe from her husband, and I want you safe from heartbreak. Staying here will be the safest thing for you and for us, however—"

He cut her off before she could go on. "I do not think you need protection."

To accent his point, Matthias looked around at the potions, poisons, and other things he did not know but suspected to be vile. He had no idea what they were used for, he simply had a bias against all things witchcraft.

Juniper couldn't blame him, not after what witchcraft had done to him. *But it is people like him—people who cannot accept that it is not all good nor all evil—who are at the root of witch burnings.* Juniper stopped spinning her tea. "When you were young, Mama was ra—"

Matthias flinched. "I know, Juniper."

"And out of that came me. Why she kept me, I will never know... but I am grateful. When you left, someone tried to burn the house down as we slept inside. I would have died had it not been for Mama. She nearly died, saving my life. People are growing braver, and there are attacks every other week—what we can do is no longer protecting us. The witch hunts around the world are inspiring people in town, and we need protection."

"Won't you have a Wolf?" Matthias asked.

"You need to leave Ocleau, take the moon curse, and learn to live with it. Because if you stay..." She looked down at her tea, the steam billowing before her. "Tell me the truth, Matthias, do you love Ana? Or will you be able to stick around and face Mama when she sends Ana's husband to rip out her throat? Because Mama is going to make you watch her new pet kill Ana. To ensure your loyalty, Ana will likely be her husband's first victim."

Matthias's flinch told Juniper everything she needed to know. He always did his best to conceal his secrets, but he only lasted so long before something made him spill. Juniper knew the right words to make him slip. The death of a woman he loved—or one he believed he may come to love—was the one thing that kept him up at night. Juniper heard him talking in his sleep.

She reached over and held his sturdy hands in hers. "You should leave while you still can."

He leaned his head to the side, sadness in his gray eyes. "I can't leave Ana or..."

"Your daughter," Juniper whispered. *He's planning on putting his family back together with Ana in Riina's stead.*

Matthias nodded weakly. "I need the curse out of me so I can take them away from here. Please, Juniper, I beg you. Do not tell Azalea."

"I fear for you," she said as she got to her feet. She cast one more look at her brother before retiring to her bedroom. She could not look at him any longer; the agony ripped her apart. Either he stayed, and his life was torn to shreds, but she would have her brother back. Or he fled now, and she would never see him again.

Azalea

Juniper

Matthias — Rima

Elise

PART III
The Wolf

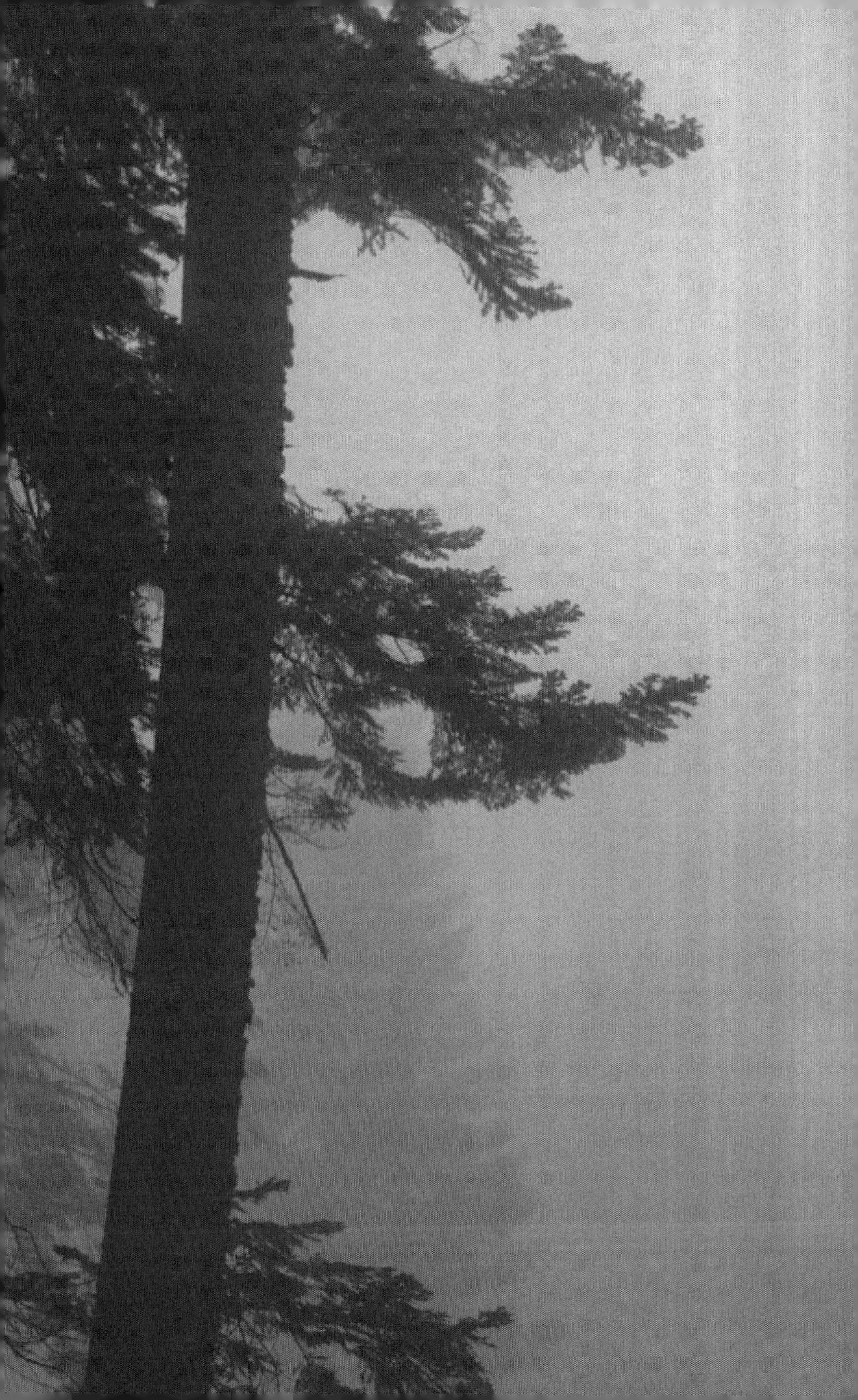

21

OCLEAU

THE YEAR OF THE CURSE

BLAEZ

Night swept over the forest. Owls called out a beautiful, ghostly sound. No bugs tittered in the trees, the night almost entirely silent except for an animal hunting in the dark, the owls, and a lonely hunter snapping twigs and tossing them into the crackling fire. Only mere inches away from his boots, the warmth sank into him.

From this vantage point, with his back against a giant spruce tree and the firelight illuminating the grove where he camped, Blaez could see everything he needed to see. But nothing out here would harm him; he spent half his life hunting in these woods. Every life he took, he offered thanks as he put it out of its misery. The pain of watching a terrified animal look at him for help when he was the cause of its suffering never sat right with him. But he needed food and clothing, and not a single part of any animal killed went to waste: marrow for soup, bones for fertilizer and fashioned into trinkets and jewelry to sell, pelts for warmth during the long, cold winters in Ocleau.

Blaez reached his hand up to his cheek, feeling the faint scratches with the calloused pads of his fingers. They were almost healed. With a heavy sigh, he leaned forward and rubbed his chest with his hands to keep warm, then hoisted a large bear pelt over his body. In a few days, he would return to his homestead with a surplus of items for Ana to use and sell to keep her happy. To keep her occupied.

Running his hand over his bearded face, Blaez shut his eyes tight. He didn't want to go home. He could barely call that place home. It was never his; he had never been welcomed there. He was a guest, no matter how often he patched the holes in the roof or reinforced the walls so they would not fall to ruin. Returning to Ocleau was something he dreaded so deeply that he considered never going back. But he had already been gone for over a week, the longest he had ever been. His return could not be delayed any longer.

A war went on inside his chest—a battle within his heart for what he knew was right and for what he wanted. While he knew returning home would lead to more abuse, he couldn't stop loving Ana, no matter how hard he tried. When he fell in love with her, he sensed that she possessed a dark side, but he never expected it to come out the way it did. They met shortly after her parents died of a vicious plague that had run rampant through the town, slimming a population already decimated by a brutal winter. Blaez understood her circumstances but thought asking her hand in marriage would have been taking advantage of her situation.

When Ana suggested the idea, he agreed, not just to help her, but because he'd fallen helplessly in love with her. In the beginning, she showed affection only when she wanted to. Blaez couldn't help but notice she lacked something that would have allowed her to love him in return. No matter what he offered—space, fine jewelry, to be at her beck and call—it was never enough. It was as though she looked for something in him that he would never have.

She laid with him on her terms, which Blaez accepted. To show he loved her and wanted the best for her, he never pushed anything on her. But after some time, they knew that she could not bear children, which Blaez had hoped might bring out that missing piece of her. When he asked her about it, she agreed to try other methods to increase their chances of getting pregnant.

Blaez thought it was he who could not give her what she wanted. Until the miscarriage. It was then that Blaez sought out a young woman adept in healing. With long brown hair that was board-straight and green eyes that shone like grass on a spring day, she promised an answer to their problem. She was very young at the time, at most fifteen, but she was confident in her skills. At a cost that forced Blaez to nearly break his back with work to make up for it, he returned with an herbal tea that would help Ana conceive.

Blaez never wanted a family; he didn't want to raise children, but he would do anything for her.

Ana never took it. That was when he realized she never wanted a child. Not with him, at the very least. She grew cold and mean, first with her words, then her fists. He took the abuse because that was what he was meant to do: help her through her pain. But it never stopped. It just developed into an unbridled fury.

Being barren broke something further inside her. When Ana took it out on him, Blaez hoped it would help. Whatever made her feel something, whatever she needed to do to feel better, he would weather that storm, no matter how much it made him ache. Not physically, though he had bruises and scratches from some of the worst days. Mentally, it shattered him.

This time was the last time.

"You are useless," she snapped at him a week ago. "Our sow died because you forgot to bring her in."

There was no sense in arguing. It had been his fault. But something came up from his core, bubbling to the surface. "You could have done it, Ana. I cannot be responsible for everything in this house."

"It's *my* house," she snapped back, stepping up to him. She was small but unbalanced rage burned behind her eyes.

"So, you should help," he replied, raising his voice unintentionally. Something burned behind his eyes too; he was tired of being blamed for all her problems. He was not the root of her issues; those started long before they met.

"I let you live here—I let you have my father's roof over your head. You should be groveling; you should be thankful and grateful for what I give you." She shoved him.

He barely budged, infuriating her.

"What would you have without me?" she screeched.

"Peace," he growled back at her.

She slashed at him with her nails, reaching for his hair.

Blaez stepped back, yanking himself free.

Wavering, she calculated whether to go for him again. He raised his lip with a growl, and she mimicked him. Without another word, he left the house. He didn't know what he would do if he stayed. He hated the realization that he despised Ana.

A spark flew from the fire and landed on his trousers, snapping him from his thoughts. He realized he'd been fingering the light scratches on his face again, and he knew what he must do. Being with Ana brought out the worst in her, and letting her take it out on him only enabled her to transfer her anger onto him instead of facing what troubled her head-on.

Blaez understood they were not meant to be together. Despite that, he debated leaving her, knowing she would lose the land and her home. Blaez didn't want her land; he would leave Ocleau and ensure that the land was hers entirely if it was possible, but the law stated no woman could own land. Ana's only option if he left was to become a matron at the orphanage, the sentence for every impoverished woman in the village, or to live life as a vagabond. He had stayed for her, knowing she was using him. Now, he would leave for himself.

Though he still loved her, Blaez decided that he had to leave because he hated her.

22

SILVANIA

THE YEAR OF THE MOON

SORIN

The two young witches were beginning their descent into the woods when they heard shouting from a nearby home. Here, at the edge of the forest, no houses stood close enough that they should be able to hear the screams. Tatiana and Lilianna's screams. Sorin spun quickly at the sound, knowing the voices all too well, her heart already aching for the pain her friends—her sisters—were going through. Sorin's hand jerked out, grabbing Alina's wrist and tugging the determined young woman back—she was barrelling through to get Red back, no matter the cost, but there were other lives in danger. Sorin wasn't going to let anyone lay a hand on the two ever again.

Whatever happened with the failed protection spell, it worked enough to allow Alina to see Red, possessed and being brought to the Wolf. It worked well enough to carry the screams across town so Sorin could hear them. She had to choose between the Floarea sisters and Red.

She spent hours learning about every fable and myth about the Wolf and his creator recently. *If my studies prove anything, it's that the sacrifices may have made it out unscathed,* Sorin thought. *Red has time.*

At that moment, Tatiana and Lilianna needed to be the priority.

"Alina, please," Sorin begged, still gripping her wrist.

"But Red," Alina whimpered, pulling away.

"Our sisters are being hurt as we speak!" Sorin snapped. "First, we help them. Then the four of us find Red together."

Another scream from the Floarea house made Alina gasp. She glanced toward the town line but allowed Sorin to pull her in the opposite direction. They ran as quickly as they could, the rocks slicing into the tough skin of their bare feet. Sorin saw with disbelief that other houses had their lights on, but not one tried to help the sisters. *Not one neighbor decided enough was enough and stood up for the girls. This whole town deserves to burn.*

Anger billowed inside Sorin, fanning the flames of her courage as she raced to the Floarea household. The screaming reached a fever pitch, and she yanked the front door handle. Locked. She hissed and looked around for anything to get through. She spotted an ax deeply embedded in a log. She pulled it free and marched back to the door, gripping it with the ferocity of a mother protecting her young.

Driving the ax through the door proved harder than she expected; the oak door was strong and sturdy. She raced to the windows; they showed no signs of life, but Sorin knew that the sisters were awake inside. The screaming continued, rattling Sorin's head as she swung the ax. Glass shattered as it smashed the window; she cleared the shards quickly and reached in to release the latch.

"Help me up," Sorin commanded.

Alina obeyed, boosting her through the window. She ran to the door and unlocked the bolt so Alina could come inside. Still holding the ax, she barrelled through the hallway to where she heard Tatiana shouting and Lilianna crying without looking back to see if Alina followed.

"What was that?" Sorin heard Mr. Floarea say from the girls' room. There was only a muffled whimper in reply. "Was that your little friend?"

Sorin burst through the bedroom door.

Lilianna was seated on her bed with her legs tucked up against her chest, hands over her ears, and her eyes tightly closed. Tatiana was pinned beneath her father. His hand wrapped around her chin, covering her mouth and pinning her head to the side. She saw Sorin with an ax, and a look of relief crossed her face. But their father was not surprised, for he heard the glass shattering and saw the door swing open from the corner of his eye.

Mr. Floarea turned, ready to knock her down with a single swing of his beefy arm, but his eyes widened when he spotted the ax. He hadn't expected her to wield a weapon. Shock crossed his features, and he only had time to narrow his eyes before Sorin used all her strength to bring the ax down, pulverizing Mr. Floarea's wrist. The *thunk* of the metal against bone was followed by a brutish yell of agony, making Sorin grin.

Mr. Floarea wasn't done fighting. He gripped his wounded hand; the flesh peeled back from the bone, blood gushing from the gaping laceration. He lunged for Sorin, ignoring his two children.

She swung the ax again, but he blocked it, sending it flying to the side. It scraped along the wood floors until it hit the wardrobe and stilled.

Mr. Floarea backhanded Sorin, who stumbled as blood spilled from her lower lip. She wiped the blood from her chin, streaking it along her face and giving her the appearance of a ravenous animal. Poised with the intent to kill, she braced herself for the impact as Mr. Floarea threw himself at her.

A sudden yelp made them both pause, and Sorin stared as she realized the sound came from his mouth. High-pitched at first, it turned into the whimper of a wounded dog. He craned his neck, peering over his shoulder, allowing Sorin to see the ax embedded in his lower back. Tatiana held its shaft, standing tall in her determination to protect her sister and friend.

Alina stood in the doorway, frozen in shock, as she watched Mr.

Floarea fall. He lay on the ground, bleeding profusely from the wounds on his arm and back. Only when she was sure he would not rise did she scurry around his body and embrace Lilianna, who cried silently.

Tatiana yanked the ax free, lifting it high before bringing it down again. There was a sickening squelch of flesh and blood when she made contact with his body. Blood sprayed them as she continued to strike him; even Lilianna was hit with a few droplets. Tatiana wasn't finished, so she brought the ax down again and again until the only thing left of her father was chunks. His arm was severed, his head hung by a tendon, and his fingers scattered underneath the furniture. His back looked like the notorious Wolf of Silvania had ripped him apart.

Silence filled the room when she dropped the ax and spit on her father's corpse.

Sorin looked up at Tatiana. "Thank you."

"Why didn't it work?" Tatiana asked, slightly dazed. Her heart-shaped face was covered in blood and tears.

"I do not know," Sorin replied bitterly, ashamed she was unable to promise the girls safety like she hoped. She felt like a fraud. "I think part of it worked."

"It did work," Lilianna spoke up suddenly. "How many times has he come into our room at night?"

"Since Ma died..." Tatiana replied.

"And has anyone ever come to our rescue?" Lilianna posed.

"Not until tonight," Tatiana realized. She looked at Sorin and Alina. "Maybe the protection was not to prevent him from being able to come into our room but for someone to save us."

Alina looked up, her mouth agape. "How do we protect Sorin from the town? Or me from love? We cannot kill everyone who might try to drive Sorin out. We cannot kill..." Alina trailed off.

"The Wolf has Red," Sorin told the others, attempting to divert the conversation away from Alina's negative train of thought. "If Lilianna is correct, we cannot waste any more time. We are stronger together."

23

OCLEAU

THE YEAR OF THE CURSE

AZALEA

Faded sunlight filtered through the canopy above Azalea. The rays were cold this late in the season, the insidious chill making her joints ache and reminding her that she was not as young as she once was. As she grew older, she would be less able to protect herself and Juniper. *If only Matthias's father was still alive*, she thought before chiding herself for thinking such things. Men could only do so much—but he had not been like other men. He had been kind and tender, coaxing her to unveil a part of herself she rarely allowed to show, even back then. He taught her there were two kinds of love: the mandatory love one gives to a child and a chosen love that one offers only to a partner.

Now Matthias was all she had left of him.

Azalea looked up at the sky. Her skin prickled with goosebumps as she whistled for her crow. The bird was impossibly hidden within the trees, only to be seen when he burst out with wings spread wide. A black spot against the sun, blocking it momentarily like an eclipse. Suddenly Aegidius dove and swooped with precision, landing on Azalea's shoulder.

She looked into his eyes, searching for the man she loved, and was reminded of her failure. Cold sweat crept down her neck as she thought of her inability to put Matthias's father into Aegidius's body. *What if I fail again?* She trembled at the thought. Then she shook her head. *I am a far more powerful witch now than I was then.*

"You have news for me," Azalea said, stroking his sleek feathers lovingly. She carried him to the house. The crow cawed, hopping onto the window ledge. She spread her fingers over his neck, thumbs at his throat, and bonded with the bird. Her head snapped back at an unnatural angle; Aegidius spread his wings and froze as she infiltrated his mind.

Azalea walking away from the house to go to the market. Aegidius soaring wide around the house until she was gone from sight, then perching on the window, unseen, listening. Inside voices reverberated through his hollow bones.

"You should leave while you still can."

"I can't leave Ana or..."

"Your daughter."

"I need the curse out of me so I can take them away from here. Please, Juniper, I beg you. Do not tell Azalea."

"I fear for you."

Snapping out of the vision, Azalea stared into Aegidius's eyes, hoping he was lying though she knew a familiar could not lie to its witch. She removed her hands. Her already stiff joints were near seizing; she cracked her neck to give it mobility back. But the tension did not release. "A daughter?" she whispered.

Her voice grew louder with her anger. "How can the one person I trust go behind my back?" she asked Aegidius, who cocked his head to the side in reply. Disgust made her stomach churn. Not only did Juniper know Matthias had a child, she had never revealed that information to her. "What does Juniper accomplish by trying to convince her brother to leave? Has his presence here tainted her?"

Rage boiled inside of her, enough to cause Aegidius to fly off. She stared out the open window, snarling as though everything outside the house was evil. But even those inside the house had become tainted.

"So be it. She doesn't trust me; in return, she has lost my trust. I will not let her stand in the way of my success."

As the full moon grew closer with each passing night, Azalea toiled to find a way to control the Wolf. Her rage at her children fueled her, keeping her focused. *Thankless, they are. I'll deal with them both when the time comes. For now, I must find a way to control the beast.*

The displacement curse would not be difficult for her, despite her inexperience in displacement of this magnitude. She was not worried about her ability. But as she scoured every last piece of historical information on spells and incantations, she came to the realization that she may have to create such a curse herself.

"Where to begin..." she mumbled.

Creating spells took many months, requiring focus and dedication, and Azalea only had a short amount of time before the full moon. With an exasperated sigh, she rose from her seat at the book-covered table and crossed the room. There was one book she hadn't consulted.

Her fingers found the plank of wood that deviated from the others, normally hidden by her book-laden shelves. She slid it gently to the side to reveal several neglected volumes wearing thick coats of dust.

She found it easily, blowing off the dust to reveal black script that read, *Daemonion*. It was a book she'd acquired long ago but had never had use for. Though it was a simple brown leather-bound book, the title was one that, if found by the townspeople, would be sure to cause her strife. Although Azalea was a known witch in town, she made sure to keep items that could act as proof of what she and Juniper did well hidden.

When Azalea died, the house and the Craft would be left to Juniper. She wanted her daughter to remain safe from accusing hands. Despite her daughter's betrayal, Azalea knew that in time, should things go her way, she would find a way to forgive her. *So young and protective of her brother. I should not have been so open with the girl.* She had to be more careful what she said to her now that she had proven to be compromised.

Azalea opened the book, pushing thoughts of Juniper aside. The spine groaned in effort, and dust fell from the pages, settling on Azalea's skirts and the floor around her. Most of the pages contained sketches of familiars, a witch's first companion in the Craft, an animal with the spiritual knowledge to guide a witch steadily and safely. Footnotes were scribbled in the margins, more of a journal than anything else.

Without putting the book down, Azalea reached back and felt for her chair, then fell into it. Careful of the pages, she gently flipped through the progression of the book. Mice, cats, and small birds were first. A section labeled *'trying larger animals'* brought Azalea's journey to dogs, ravens, and even deer. Some were noted as failures, others as successes. Most witches used small familiars, or birds, for they were easily concealed and inconspicuous. Larger animals like dogs and deer were protectors but not useful for stealth.

She read on.

She is dying, and I cannot lose her. Although Vaike refuses my offering of eternal life, I cannot live without her.

An image of an owl was sketched on the next page with the caption: *I have put Vaike into the body of a barn owl, and I have never seen such sadness before. Twice she tried to escape, and I've had to tie her up to prevent her from injuring herself. She will get used to it—she will learn to accept that I have given her a second chance to live. I spared her from illness.*

"Yes..." Azalea flipped through to further pages. "Putting the mind of a human into the body of an animal..."

Controlling the Wolf over the course of three days was not good enough—she wanted control of him at all times. Her Wolf would not change at the full moon but at her beck and call.

She is no longer herself, and so I have infiltrated her mind. It cost us everything, but I cannot live without her. Through trial and error, I discovered the horrifying means to success. By sacrificing our daughter, Layla, I gained control of Vaike. Perhaps she simply gave up fighting when she lost Layla, but I felt so strong. When I did the task, I was riddled with power. To have control over another being, full control... It was like nothing I had ever felt before. Vaike is bound to me now that I have this power to create and control. She no longer flies without my consent. She can no longer act on her impulses to escape.

Azalea put the book down, staring straight ahead. A dizzying feeling made her head spin. The irony of it made her chuckle sourly. Juniper may have betrayed her, but she still loved her.

"What do I want more?" Azalea wondered aloud. "A wolf in my command and my son by my side? Or nothing, just Juniper. A daughter who lied to my face. A daughter who picked Matthias over her own mother."

Azalea was faced with the brutal truth that in order to gain control of the Wolf, she would need to sacrifice Juniper. Bitterness pulsed through her.

I want power.

A piece of paper slipped out of the loose pages of the book, fluttering to the floor and making a soft scratch as it touched the ground.

Azalea stared at it for a moment before bending to pick it up.

For anyone who wishes to do the same, though I hope no one ever does, the formula is simple: whilst the silver blade is upon her throat, chant 'ego tibi dabo illam vitam accipere' three times. Dig the blade deep and with a swift thrust, and let her go without pain. Capture the blood in an oak bowl filled halfway with shaved cedar, borage, and scabiosa. Let it soak for one hour, drain the blood, then feed it to the one you wish to control.

Azalea slipped the loose paper into her skirt's folds and clutched it within the fabric. Her hand grew damp with sweat, and she grew certain the old ink would bleed. It was no matter, for the words were already branded in her mind. How could she forget three ingredients and the murder of a daughter? *My only daughter, the child who loved me... Is it worth having all the power to control the weak-minded townsfolk?*

"Yes," Azalea told herself. "She cannot be trusted."

Juniper would have to die, and Matthias would remain in Ocleau.

After all, he was her true child. Her firstborn. Her chosen child. She knew what she needed to do; a blood oath to keep him. Then she would find him a proper woman, one with which to have children, to carry on the Luca line. Riina was low-bred, and Ana could not have children. Azalea would pick a proper, suitable woman.

The door burst open, bringing in Juniper and a gust of cold wind. Her daughter let out a gasp of anger. "Those beasts!"

Azalea rose to look at Juniper, wondering if she could speak without revealing everything to her observant and keen child. But Juniper was distracted, and she was able to tuck away the book in the waistband of her skirt.

Blood dripped down Juniper's cheek from a wound just below her eye; she had yet to wipe it away.

Without a word, Azalea knew what was going on. She walked past Juniper and yanked open the door.

In the distance, two men scurried down the path, hurrying away. They were skinny and lanky, just youths.

Azalea looked up to the skies and called to Aegidius. He appeared from the treetops and dove down at the fleeing cowards. The crow pulled back his wings to slow his flight and attacked relentlessly with his sharp talons. The boys' screams were music to Azalea's ears; though it was far away, she could see them covering their faces and heads with their arms, exposing them to the assault.

After a few moments, Azalea clicked her tongue, and Aegidius pulled back.

"Thank you, Mama." Juniper's voice wavered. She wiped the blood from her face.

"Where is your brother?" Azalea asked. "He should be escorting you."

"I am fine without him by my side, Mama." She took off her coat. "He has been gone for ten years, remember?"

How many of those ten years did you know about his daughter? Azalea wanted to ask.

"And how many times have you returned home with bloody cheeks? To the house being vandalized?"

"Did you discover how to control the beast yet?" Juniper asked, completely changing the subject as she narrowed her eyes.

Azalea knew they simmered with anger at her regarding Matthias, but she had no idea what she would do to keep him. She had no idea Azalea knew of her betrayal. She had no idea that for Azalea to control the Wolf, it would cost her life.

Azalea looked away, still plagued by her decision. The Wolf would be hers, but what then? If she would be forced to make a sacrifice, then so would generations after her. An incantation that would be spoken and a price to be paid. *If I have to give up a daughter, so will everyone else who uses the Wolf.*

Azalea raised her head, her decision made. *To have everything, I will first have to lose everything.*

"Mama?" Juniper pressed, seeking an answer to her question.

"No, Juniper, we must keep looking," she lied.

24

SILVANIA

THE YEAR OF THE MOON

RED

Red looked into the black eyes of the Wolf-man, awaiting his reaction. Having asked him to slaughter more than half of her family, she expected more from him than a blank stare, but that was all she received. Releasing the breath she held, Red allowed her frustration to seep out. "It is rude to ignore a person who is standing before you and speaking to you."

"No," he said, lifting his head and looking at the ceiling.

"No?" Red felt her heart sink. Her only chance at getting revenge on the people who harmed her throughout her whole life was quickly slipping through her fingers. She held tight to it, refusing to let go of the power just within her grasp. Wolf or not, she was going to do this.

"Revenge..." he gasped at the air as if trying to breathe in the words. "It does...terrible things to people."

Red did something she had never done before; she hiked up her skirt in front of a man. She had never exposed herself to anyone before. She showed him the dark bruises on her knees, large and purple, with green around the edges. Her knobby knees were warped from years of torture, and she was bone thin from all the meals she had been denied over the years. She allowed him enough time to see the damage to her body in the firelight. She watched his face as he studied her, then released the fabric and let it flow back down around her legs. She rolled up her sleeve and showed the faint marks from where she was grabbed by her father and thrown into her room. The scars on her cheeks were faded but still visible.

"I have never not been marked by abuse. I have never not ached when I woke in the mornings," she stated. Her voice quivered, both in rage and in her desire to never again be harmed by her abusers. "I have never not been *afraid*."

His expression became pained, and he dropped his head. His black eyes seemed sympathetic to her plight but nothing more. "No."

He stepped out of the house, saying nothing else. *Should I leave and return home?* she wondered. *No, I can't go across the town line, and I certainly will not return home. There is nothing left for me there.*

Either she had to kill her father and grandmother on her own, or she had to start walking. She wondered how far she could get before collapsing from cold and exhaustion. As the minutes crawled by, Red realized she was on her own. Her shoulders sagged in defeat. As much as she wanted the power to hurt those who hurt her, she did not have it on her own. Dejected and defeated, Red looked around the modest cabin. There was one room attached to the main area, and she gravitated towards it with only a single glance back to see if the man would return. Perhaps he had stepped out for a bundle of firewood or a breath of fresh air. Red suspected he didn't want to be around her after she begged him to murder for her.

In the darkness of the second room, Red fumbled for a lantern. She found it and lit it quickly, the glow of the flames spreading along the walls of the room to set the shadows dancing like witches. An unmade bed was pressed against the wall, and beside it, tucked under the window, was a beautiful desk made from rich wood. As she moved closer, she discovered a stack of parchment filled with crude charcoal sketches.

She gingerly lifted the first few pages, scratched so heavily with the charcoal that it had ripped in the center. She soon found herself entranced. Underneath each sheet, there was another with something more visible past the frantic sketching. The further she went, inspecting each sheet, she began to unveil the secrets. Beneath each crossed out and scribbled on parchment was a face; it soon became clear that it was the face of a woman. Red assumed the final sheet would be an undamaged portrait, but she did not go straight to it, continuing to unbury her page by page.

She carefully placed each piece of paper to the side. An eye appeared, wide and full of love. Next, she made out the round nose, button-like. The shape of the face took hold, beautifully round, with a soft chin to match her petite nose. As the pile grew thinner, she suddenly grew weary. The face staring back at her was unsettlingly familiar. Her stomach twisted as she reached the bottom, and she pulled forth the ancient, tea-colored parchment.

It was her.

Red's hand shook as she gripped the undamaged piece of parchment; it was like staring into a mirror.

How long has the Wolf been watching me?

Before she turned to confront the man and demand an explanation, she spotted something scrawled at the bottom. Hardly legible from the aged charcoal, the brief script, written by an untrained hand, formed a name.

Ana.

Red didn't recognize the name, the parchment still trembling in her fingers. With an unevenness to her walk, Red emerged from the bedroom and walked into the living room, where the man stood, facing the fire.

"Who is she?" Red asked.

"The woman I loved," he replied. His voice was much smoother than before, as though he found it in his brief disappearance.

"Why does she..."

"Look just like you?" He turned to face her. The defeated and sympathetic look on his face fit him so well, it was as though he always looked that way. As though for four hundred years, he had been in mourning. "I have been asking myself the same question since I first saw you."

"When *did* you first see me?" she asked, afraid to hear the answer. Was this man stalking her? Maybe he was not the Wolf after all, but someone who cowered in the woods and remained hidden from sight, watching the young girls who dared wander into the forest without protection.

"Tonight," he replied.

"Is she the reason you do not want to help me achieve my revenge? To be free of my abusers? What does she have to do with me? What does her death have to do with you being too cowardly to help?" Red added hints of guilt, hoping that by looking like the woman he loved, he would eventually help her. She was abusing his weakness, but she pushed back her conscience. With each accusatory word, she felt more power over him.

"I have enough blood on my hands." He pointed to the paper in Red's grip. "Including hers."

25

OCLEAU

THE YEAR OF THE CURSE

MATTHIAS

The crunch of the frozen gravel sounded like bones snapping as Matthias walked to the far end of town, where the poorest lived. As the houses went from humble with vast farmland to shacks with holes in the roof, Matthias kept his head down to avoid looking at it. He couldn't offer support since he had no money, but he also believed that the people who lived there were not to be pitied; they simply did not put in the effort to make their lives better. If they worked harder, they could repair the holes in their roofs and keep their families from starving.

He refused to feel bad for them, even when he reminded himself that Riina also came from this part of town. Had she not been murdered by Azalea, Matthias would have given her the world. A big house she would have gotten lost in—she would have loved that. A field where she could wander under the warmth of the summer sun. A covered porch where she could have painted everything she saw, from the deer that casually wandered into the field to the owls that perched, watching with wide, wise eyes.

Tears lined the edges of his vision, and he used the back of his hand to roughly wipe them away. The orphanage came into sight, two stories tall, rickety, and groaning under the many little feet running too fast for the matrons to keep up. He knew the children inside were either unwanted or both their parents were dead. Azalea could have prevented these children from being conceived, born or even prevented the death of their parents if they had gone to her. Matthias walked up the stairs, casting the thoughts aside.

With a jingle, the friendly-sounding bell chimed, alerting the matrons inside. He waited patiently, but it took some time for the door to open, leaving Matthias with his emptiness. He glanced down to see a young blonde child, her blue eyes like saucers, as she gazed up at the strange man on the doorstep.

"Good morning," Matthias said as he crouched down to be on her level.

She ran off the moment he settled into position.

Matthias sighed and stood back up as the matron approached him.

She had long, mousy brown hair that reached the middle of her back. Frizzed and messy, it looked as though she never took care of her own appearance, but she still possessed a subtle, simple beauty.

An idea struck Matthias. Azalea was going to make him kill Ana, but anyone could look like Ana if she were mauled badly enough. All he had to do was keep his head clear and make certain Azalea did not catch on to him. Once everything was in place and Ana and his daughter were safe, he would do what needed to be done. Everything hung from a fine thread, threatening to snap at any misstep. Another piece of his complicated plan was falling into place.

"My name is Matthias," he said, introducing himself. "You may be too young to remember me." She looked as old as Juniper.

"I remember you," she said. "Though I was still quite young the last time we saw you. Everyone here remembers you."

He forced a smile. Did she remember because of his relationship with Riina, or did she remember because he was blamed for her death? "May I... May I see her?"

The woman squinted.

"Please…I was forced out of this town and unable to take her with me." Matthias dropped his head to hide the lies in his eyes. "We wanted nothing more than to raise her, but we knew something was amiss. If I had known that she would have drowned herself—" The lie made his stomach twist, but now was not the time to point fingers at Azalea. He needed her. He pointed that finger before, and no one believed him. "I would have taken my family far away from here."

"Riina was always a complicated woman; even as a child, she did such strange things. Playing with a girl she claimed was her sister. At least, that is what I have been told," she said at last, brushing her frazzled hair behind her ear. "We have looked for similar traits in her child."

"A sister?" Matthias frowned. *Could Riina have had a sister?*

The woman shrugged. "Come, I'll take you to your daughter."

"Thank you…" Matthias paused, allowing a moment for it to feel authentic, when he asked, "What is your name?"

"Kaisa," she replied.

"Kaisa…?"

"Kaisa Tamm," she said with a smile, then beckoned for him. "Come in, Matthias Luca."

They wandered the labyrinth of hallways, bedrooms, and children underfoot. Matthias kept himself carefully composed as he followed behind her, observing everything from wailing babies to young ladies who looked nearly old enough to end up in a brothel or as a matron within the year. None of the young girls raised in the orphanage became well-bred women. In Matthias and Riina's case, they were both young and fell in love too quickly—he was her chance at a perfect life. But he hadn't been swift enough in taking her away from this place. Matthias vowed he would not make the same mistake with Ana.

A large common room littered with soiled blankets, straw dolls missing limbs, and too many children came into sight. It took

Matthias two seconds to find his daughter, her soft brown hair tied up in braids around her head and her warm, doe-like eyes looking for more than her dreary life. Guilt tore at him, but he knew her only other option would have been his mother. Azalea most certainly would have killed her—or worse, made her a witch.

It was Matthias's choice to leave their daughter here, promising to come back for her. Riina was scarcely out of the orphanage when she had their daughter and knew that it was not an ideal place to grow up, but she wanted to better her own life before caring for another. Both had agreed Azalea could not know about Eliise, and the orphanage was the only place that seemed safe. They had plans to move to a neighboring town—any town away from Azalea would do—build a home, then come back for their child.

"Eliise," Kaisa called to the young girl. Matthias never had a chance to learn her name; Riina hadn't named her before she died. She wanted to name her everything and nothing, no name was suitable, and she hadn't made a decision in time. Eliise. It sounded right. Kaisa told the girl, "There is someone here to see you."

The girl looked up, her eyes scanning until they landed on Matthias. No recognition flashed through them; of course, she would not remember him. She was only a few weeks old when Matthias left Ocleau. She stood, wiping dust and crumbs from her beige skirt before daintily walking over to her father.

"Are you here to take me away?" she asked, a hint of desperation in her voice.

"Not yet." Matthias crouched down and cupped her face. Her eyes resembled her mother's, a rich, deep brown. The color of tea steeped too long. "Soon, I will come for you and give you the life you have always dreamed of."

"Do not give her false hope," Kaisa scolded.

"I do no such thing," Matthias replied. "Eliise, I am your father. I have been away for a very long time. I was forced to leave you behind.

But now I have returned, and I will take you far away from here. You have my word."

Eliise stared blankly at him, unsure how to digest his promises. She glanced at Kaisa, looking for confirmation of Matthias's words.

Kaisa said nothing; clearly, she didn't trust him to follow through. After all, he abandoned his child for ten years.

"What would you like to do? What has been your dream?" Matthias asked her.

"To see Mama."

Matthias smiled; even if Eliise could remember, Ana looked just like Riina. They wanted the same thing, Matthias and Eliise. They both wanted Ana. This time, he would not let Azalea take that away from him or Eliise again. Everything was falling into place. He could feel it. "I can do that. I promise I'll bring you to your mother very soon."

She smiled tentatively, then wrapped her arms around Matthias's neck in a weak-armed hug.

Matthias left the orphanage with questions burning in his mind. *Am I capable of having Kaisa, an innocent, killed in replacement of Ana?* Everyone believed him to be so righteous and yet the idea of letting Kaisa be a stand-in for Ana's corpse came so easily. *Too easily*, he thought as he walked the long way around town to Ana's house.

The second, more important question would soon be answered.

His urgency moved him along quicker than usual. In the dense fog that crept in as the hour grew late, he found himself momentarily lost. Only the skeletal trees on his right guided him. He had visited Ana nearly every day since his mother poisoned her with sickness. He tended to her, and every moment he was there, he feared her husband would return.

Her house came into sight, and Matthias relaxed. The decaying head of winter rose on the doorstep, reminding him that he was an interloper here. This was Ana and her husband's home. The rose was a symbol of their deceit. He knocked on the door, prepared to face the man of the house at any time. When no one answered, he presumed it was safe and entered. The bitter scent of bile and an unwashed body told Matthias that only Ana was home. He quickly hurried to check on her.

Ana's eyes fluttered open when Matthias entered the bedroom. She attempted a smile but winced in obvious pain. "What are you doing here?" she croaked as she sat up.

"I need to ask you something," he said, as he sat on the side of the bed. Before she could reply, he continued, "You spoke of Riina as though you knew her. Was she—"

"My half-sister," Ana replied. "Banned from my home by my mother, who was ashamed of my father's infidelity. We still played as much as we could…until one day, she was no longer around."

"Why?" Matthias asked. His hands were sweating, and he wiped them on his trousers.

Her eyes, surrounded by bruised skin, searched until they landed on a cup.

Matthias handed it to her, and she drank small sips.

When she finished, she gave it to Matthias, who gripped it tight.

"She met you."

Matthias inhaled sharply. More questions pummeled him inside. *Did she ever see Riina again?* he wondered. Instead, he asked, "Did you know she had a child?"

Ana nodded. "Not right away, but not long after you fled Ocleau. I could do nothing for the girl, so I didn't take her in. Besides, she wasn't mine to take."

"You knew who I was when we met, and you knew I had a child." Matthias tapped his fingers on the edge of the cup. "Ana, is that… something you want?"

She coughed, her entire body shuddering at the effort. When she recovered, she took the water from him again. After she finished what was left, she wiped her mouth with the back of her hand. "When I was younger, I always wanted what she had."

"And now?"

"I'm sure you know more than most that Riina understood love in a profound way." Ana looked up and held his gaze. She grabbed his hand weakly in hers. "I want what she had."

26

SILVANIA

THE YEAR OF THE MOON

RED

Red stood, stunned. His guilt was etched onto his face; she noticed his pain the moment she saw him but now understood what lurked behind those coal-black eyes. His remorse made Red back down for a moment. *But I need Grandmother dead. Father, too,* she thought.

"I am sorry," she said.

"It is not you who made me do it; you have nothing to be sorry about." If he meant the words to be comforting, he failed, for they came out as vicious. "And you do not want blood on your hands. I promise it will not make you feel better."

Red didn't believe him, and she lifted her lip in protest, no longer caring about how sad or guilty he was. *He has no idea what I've suffered. How could he? He's a man,* she thought. *He didn't suffer at the hand of anyone before he became the Wolf.* She pointed at him with her free hand, the other still clutching the shaking parchment. "My own father sacrificed me to you, knowing that you could kill me, rape me, do whatever you wanted to me—"

"I wouldn—"

"He did not care! He didn't care what you might do to me," Red shouted at him. "My grandmother's favorite pastime is to see how hard she can strike me, how long she can make me work until my back aches, how long I can kneel on a stick before sobbing. Do you have any idea what that is like? Do you have no sympathy for the abused? Will you just turn your head like everyone else in this town?" She spat the words at him, fire in her eyes.

His black eyes did not waver. Then his shoulders dropped, and his head followed suit. Looking up with his head cast down, he muttered, "Very well."

Satisfaction filled Red, her thirst for vengeance finally promised its deepest desire.

She tightened the strings of her cloak and pulled the hood over her matted hair. The man added two more logs to the fire, causing spiders to scuttle in panic as they faced the flames. Then he opened the front door wordlessly, and stepped out into the night.

Red hurried after him, closing the door behind her to seal in the heat, though she had no idea if she would see this place again. As they walked into the woods toward her grandmother's house, Red glanced back.

With the warm orange glow coming from the two visible windows, the lone cabin in the woods looked like a fragment of a child's imagination. A shiver ran down the length of her spine as the nipping winter cold hit her skin once again. The crunch of the man's footsteps over leaves and sticks soothed her. It reminded her that it was out here where she harvested her power.

"The moon is full, how is it you are a man?" Red asked.

"I'm not quite a wolf or man, nor am I just a werewolf," he said. "When I was bound to this curse, the moon no longer controlled me. Whenever the curse is enacted, I shift and do what I'm summoned for. Outside of that, I can shift when I wish. Sometimes I live as a man, other times I live as a wolf."

"How did you come to be this...the Wolf?" Red asked.

Overhead, the clouds blotted out most of the moon, faint patches allowing brief sightings that cast an ashen tone to their skin. The man looked at her, meeting her eyes like they were equals. "A series of events that I had little control over. Putting my trust in the wrong people."

Red scoffed. "That is hardly an answer."

"What will you do after you've killed your family?" His question hung in the air, a brutal accusation.

She grimaced, looking at the ground as she carefully stepped over a gnarled root. Her thoughts moved to the other girls, Sorin, Alina, Lilianna, and Tatiana. *I want to be with them, I want to live amongst them like a coven without worrying about being hit, starved, locked away...sacrificed.*

But such a dream was just that, a dream. In this world, witches and women didn't get those types of choices. They didn't get to live those kinds of free lives. That was for men.

"Will you allow me to leave?" she asked.

He glanced up at the moon. "I have no say in what you will or will not do."

"Tell me about the curse," she suggested. "And I will tell you what I will do with my freedom."

He sighed, releasing a few hundred years of remorse. The knitted anger in the creases above his brows relinquished its hold on him, making way for despair. "A daughter is sacrificed, given to me for whatever I want. A name is whispered into the wind, and I have no control after that moment. Although I can see everything, I cannot stop myself as the shift takes over, as my bones break and bend. The hunger...it comes, and I cannot control it, driven to the name that has been called. I am not proud of what I have done, but I know that there is nothing I can do to stop it. I am used to end bloodlines, but I was mercifully forgotten for two hundred years. Until now. I only know this time, something went wrong because I should have killed whomever your father wanted dead by now."

Red shot a glance at him from the side, but he did not see it. "What happens to the daughters?"

"What do the stories tell you? What did your mother tell you?"

"That he...you defile them and eat them afterward." Red blushed at how silly it sounded. *This man is no real killer; just because he's murdered bloodlines, there isn't a bone in his body that wanted to.*

Another wave of guilt hit her as she remembered where she was taking him and the reason why she dragged him along like a dog on a leash, pulling tight so the chain dug into his throat and suffocated him. Maybe she was no different from everyone else who came before her.

He let out an ugly chuckle, full of disgust. "Marie Dalca lived in Ocleau for forty-three years before her death of old age. Gabriela Sala lived for twenty-three before she died of the plague. Magda Funar lived for sixty-seven years, one town over. Narcisa Bălan disappeared from this ugly town with a young man, they married and had several children. I don't touch them. I don't do anything except give them something better in life, a way out from the family that would give them up to have me murder for them. Cowards. All of them."

"I did not know..."

"They never consider for a moment that maybe I do not like the killing, the spilling of innocent—or not so innocent—blood. I've killed fathers, mothers, children, infants... I look at my hands and see they are stained. They will always be stained. The only way I can sleep —when I do manage to sleep—is by knowing that the sacrificed lead the best lives they can because of me. I do not take all the credit, no, but I do help them." Anger dripped from his words.

"Is that why you are helping me?" she asked.

He glared at her. "I may not be innocent, and I am far from being righteous, but what you are asking me to do is evil. You're asking me to kill by choice."

Red looked ahead and spotted the familiar house, overpowering her, so she felt insignificant under its gaze. "You saved all those girls—why can't you see this as saving me?"

"I can get you out of this town..."

"I said I would tell you what I would do with my freedom. I would bring peace to Silvania. I don't want to leave and start a new life elsewhere; I want to rid the town of its evil and let something else bloom from the ashes. We have to change. We must make them see. Do you understand? For all of us, for you...it must change. My story is not new."

"As long as I am here, the town will never stop being evil," he muttered.

Silence lingered as they stood before the house, knowing what came next.

27

OCLEAU

THE YEAR OF THE CURSE

BLAEZ

Returning home was always troublesome for Blaez. He never knew how Ana would be when he returned: pleased to see him back with meat and furs carried over his shoulders or displeased that he was still alive and hadn't been mauled during his hunt? She was unpredictable, but so long as he stayed out of her way, he could get through unscathed. One wrong word, one wrong action, and she would unleash her fury upon him.

The fields of their land—her land—came into sight. Spiderwebs glittered in the morning dew, and stretched over the fences. His verdant eyes surveyed the frost that coated the grass, making it look almost blue in the sunlight. In the distance, he could see the goats and cows. They seemed in high spirits, better than himself. *The simplest of animals lived the happiest of lives*, he thought. *Only humans could suffer as much as they do, as though they want it. Maybe that was why I stay with Ana—to suffer is to be alive.*

The knobby legs of the deer hung over either shoulder, his hands clutching onto its muscular haunches. Blaez walked with a slow grace through the field, avoiding his own animals to keep from spooking them with the scent of death in the air. Overhead, a weak plume of smoke rose from the chimney, suggesting Ana was home. The white color blended into the clouds, letting him know the fire had long gone out.

His chest constricted as he approached their home. He wondered what Ana would do when he told her he was leaving her, and the thought made him stop in his tracks. Suddenly the weight of the deer became too heavy, and he dropped to a knee to collect himself. *Why do I come back? Why do I always come back?* He mocked himself for not being man enough to leave. *Coward.* The word throbbed in his skull.

With a grunt of exertion, he climbed back to his feet and went to the overhang on the west side of the house, where his tools for skinning hung against the wall. Their polished glint winked at him. He took pride in his work, in his ability and skill at many trades. But still, the thump of the corpse as he unloaded it onto the table weighed heavy on his heart. He stroked the coarse hair over the beast's torso. "Thank you," he whispered.

Blaez went to work, setting out a bucket to collect the viscera, then removing its fur and skin with his paring knife. He hung the thin layer of skin over taut strings to dry, then trimmed each cut with careful precision. Butchering the deer took a long time, and though it was filthy work, it calmed Blaez enough to face Ana and the domestic troubles that often awaited him at home. Using a metal basin filled with icy water, he washed the blood from his hands, though they would remain a reddish tint for a few days, then splashed the cold water over his dirty, bearded face. Using a clean knife, Blaez tidied himself up, shaving to reveal the soft flesh hidden beneath his beard.

He opened his front door with cautious silence and was greeted with the pungent stench of sickness. His nose wrinkled as his eyes surveyed the room. He noted an untouched pot of tea, the leaves bloated and swollen, giving off the scent of faded mint and lavender. It was not enough to cover the stench. Something was very wrong. *Maybe*, he thought bitterly with a hint of excitement, *Ana is dead.* Disgusted by his thoughts, he quickly headed toward the bedroom.

He found Ana in the bed, shivering on her side with a bucket of vomit, some of it caked on her cheek. Blaez was immediately pummeled with guilt over leaving her for a week and allowing her to fall sick while he was away. If he had been home, he might have been able to prevent her from falling ill. Perhaps she had overexerted herself or exposed herself to the elements when Blaez should have been there to do it instead.

"Ana."

She barely stirred at his voice.

"I'm so sorry. I should never have left," he said. An unusual sense of superiority suddenly came over him; Ana deserved to fall ill for all she had done. But smugness did not come naturally to him, and it faded fast. It was overpowered by his need to help her, as he had done so many times before.

A memory hit suddenly, a different time, a different illness...

He had returned home in a similar fashion, filthy from hunting but with the spoils of a successful trip. He entered the house to greet the scent of blood, strong and bitter to his nostrils. He found Ana sitting on the bed. Blood drenched the blankets, covering her hands held between her legs up to the wrists. She took a few moments to notice him. Her stare was so blank, he wasn't sure if she saw him or if she was so overpowered by grief. She'd lost a child they hadn't even known she carried.

He tried to comfort her then, but she clawed at him. The attack only lasted a few seconds before she collapsed into him. He carried her to the tub and bathed her, washing all the blood away, but he could not wash away her pain. He could not erase the sorrow she carried inside her after that.

After Blaez had gotten her cleaned up, he stripped the bed of the blood-soaked linens and burned them—he would not be able to sleep on those sheets even if they could be cleaned. He dressed Ana, who was still catatonic, in fresh clothes and gave her a drink to soothe her insides—tea with whiskey to ease the mental and physical pain. She drank silently. It prevailed for three days before he finally suggested they speak to someone who could help. If Ana wanted a child, Blaez would do what he could to get it for her.

That was when he found the young woman, the daughter of a witch, who called herself Juniper.

Blaez snapped out of his memory and focused on the reality he was being forced to face—his wife, bedridden and near death based on her emaciated cheekbones and the dried blood crusted at the corners of her lips. Blaez knew he needed to take drastic measures to cure her of what ailment she caught while he was away. *I cannot leave her like this.*

Not caring if her sickness was contagious, he knelt by the side of the bed and brushed the sweat-matted hair out of Ana's face, gently speaking her name to get her attention.

"Blaez?" she croaked.

"Ana." He breathed in relief. She was still conscious. Disappointment laughed at him deep down.

"Ana, tell me what has happened."

"Help..." She winced in pain, then forced her eyes open to look at him. Her cracked white lips parted; her breath reeked of vomit. "G-go to...*her*."

Blaez didn't need to ask who she meant. He thought of the unused brew he spent his last coin on all those years ago. The thought of it soured his thoughts. This year had not proven bountiful, but everyone knew the witch dealt in more than coin. He wondered what this was going to cost him.

He brushed her hair back again, then stood to fetch a bucket of water. He warmed it over the fire, then with a dampened cloth, he cleaned Ana's face, dabbing away at blood-streaked vomit residue. Panic struck him, but he kept his face calm so he wouldn't scare her. She had to be scared already; who knew how long she had been in such a wretched state.

After he cleaned her up, he draped her with a blanket to make her comfortable, swapped out the bucket, and left her a cup of water. There was no time to waste, for half the day had already come and gone. Blaez put on his coat. He placed a gentle hand on Ana's shoulder, then leaned down to kiss her forehead. A swell of love filled him, and he knew that he would not leave her, no matter how hard she hit him, no matter what vicious words she would spit at him as soon as she could. He was weak, he knew, but he prided himself on knowing his love for her was strong and undying.

Yet the hatred still lingered, lurking beneath the love. He would not allow it to surface; he would not allow her to see it during her moments of weakness. He forced it down, accepting that he did love Ana.

"I will fix this," he whispered before he left.

28

SILVANIA

THE YEAR OF THE MOON

THE WOLF

He stood before the skeleton of a house, ominous in the woods. It reminded him of another home—one he'd last seen long ago but still burned clearly in his memory. A similarly tall structure, crooked from years of neglect, blackened over time... How eerily similar it was to the derelict house Azalea had lived in. It made him shudder. He glanced at the young woman dressed in a red cloak, realizing there was no going back from this—for either of them.

Perhaps it will be easier this way. If what she told him was true, that this woman was evil...maybe it would come naturally to him. *All I have to do is shut my eyes and pretend it's Azalea. Would it be easier?*

No, it wouldn't.

"Are you sure about this?"

She looked at him. "I have never been so sure about anything in my life."

She doesn't understand what comes after killing—the guilt, the self-loathing, the nightmares. He wanted to protect her from it. Some people got blood on their hands and liked the taste of it—he couldn't allow her to go down that path. He spent four hundred years trying to forget what he had done; when had he last slept without nightmares?

He realized, as he looked at the young woman who looked so much like Ana that he didn't know what to call her. "What is your name?"

"Red." She smiled. "Have you remembered yours?"

He dug for the answer, but it refused to surface. *All the killing, all the dead... I remember every one of them.* With each person slaughtered by his hand, he lost a part of himself. He no longer knew how to identify. *I am nothing more than the Wolf.* He shook his head in response.

How many years had he spent living as one? Shifting into that beastly form, letting his animal instincts take over? No matter what form he took, it was the loneliness that plagued him. As a man, he was not welcome in the town; he could not even step foot over its border unless called upon as the Wolf, and then only to kill. In Wolf-form, no other packs welcomed him; his presence had long since driven any other wolves out of the area. He sensed them creeping along the edges of the forest, waiting for him to leave so they could return. But he was tethered here by the scroll; wherever it went, so did he.

Red walked up the stairs and placed her hand on the doorknob. He made a swift movement and was at her side in an instant, his hand atop hers to stop her from twisting it.

"You cannot change my mind," she said. "All you can do is help me —or leave."

He frowned. To kill one more person, someone who Red claimed was evil, would hopefully not take anything more from him. There was scarcely anything left to take. He would take the blame, as he always did. The chill from her skin crawled into him from where their hands touched, and he dropped his hand.

He studied her determined face, wondering if she was right. The town needed to change, if it *could* change. Maybe she was the one to set the chain of events into motion. Maybe all she needed was someone to help her onto that path.

"I will do it for you."

Surprise and relief showed on her face. A flicker of something wicked flashed behind her brown eyes, then quickly softened. "Thank you."

She stepped aside to let him through the door she held open.

He glanced up through the porch overhang, riddled with holes, and wondered if this would be the start of a new era. After all, the century was almost over. The moment word spread that the Wolf was being used again, it would strike fear in hearts all over town, and diabolical people would soon fight for the scroll. If there was anything he'd learned in his centuries of life, it was that history always repeats itself.

Unless Red can stop it. Even if there was darkness in her, a power-hungry creature lurking under the gentle façade, perhaps it could be prevented from rising. *If I do this for her, perhaps it will quench her desire for blood.*

Her family's murder would not go unnoticed. The townspeople would string her up from the first tree they found. The thought of her hanging from a noose, her feet kicking, and hands scrambling to remove the thick rope squeezing the life from her throat was enough for him to walk through the door.

He stepped into the house. Not a single candle was lit inside, and he was thankful. Hopefully, Red would not be able to see him clearly. The process—though he couldn't truly witness it—was horrific.

"Avert your eyes," he growled.

Red complied, remaining on the front porch and shutting the door.

He quickly removed his trousers, folded them, and placed them on a small table. His night-adjusted eyes saw every obstacle, and his nose picked up the scent of sickness in the far room. Red's grandmother was too stubborn to die; he could taste that in the air. The stale scent of mildew hardly covered the odor of approaching death.

Allowing himself to make the change, he let out a groan of pain as his bones began to crack, his spine shortening and his elbows twisting. Collapsing to the floor, he thought he heard someone call to him, but he could not look. His eyes were shut tight as the transformation took over, thick hair springing from every inch of his flesh, his skull stretching and forming into a beastly snout. All at once it was over, and he was left panting, the pain a haunting memory, and nothing more.

He could smell Red's fear, but he did not look back at her. Instinct kicked in, bringing with it the desire to kill the weakest in the area, and that was the elderly woman sleeping in the bedroom. He could smell her strongly now, so close to death, so close to decay. Lumbering through the house with effortless grace, he weaved through the furniture, dust billowing up around him. The bedroom door was left open a crack; his snout fit in, and he nudged it open with his robust shoulders. Drool dripped from his jowls, followed by a deep, carnal growl.

The woman woke, jerking upright. She recognized the creature of legend immediately, and the deep-set fear that had been with her for her entire life bubbled up as her face contorted, mouth parting, and eyes bulging. She scrambled out on the other side of the bed, searching frantically for a weapon, but found only the glass lantern beside her bedside. Hoisting it over her head, she lobbed it at him, missing the sleek black wolf by half a meter.

"Get back, beast!" she howled.

His long claws clattered against the floor, his haunches prepared to lunge, his tail low and hair on end. His maw parted wide to show a seemingly endless row of sharp teeth before he made the leap. His powerful muscles sent him straight across the room, his front paws knocking the woman down and pinning her to the ground. She opened her mouth to scream as he brought his jaws down over her throat, biting through the soft, wrinkled flesh and ripping everything apart. He felt her arteries split and tear, blood soaking the floor and his black fur.

Her scream never made it out, a silent memory in his mind for the rest of time.

When he was sure she was dead, he backed off and transformed back to man. Stumbling through the house, naked and covered in blood, he wiped his face with the back of his forearm and reached for his trousers. He stepped into them, then took a deep breath, trying to calm himself down before he saw Red.

He regained his composure, but not that last piece of himself he lost in the bedroom. *I guess there was something left of me to take,* he thought.

He stumbled out onto the porch to face the young woman, her wide eyes swimming with a combination of fear and excitement. Her lips parted ever so slightly, as though she was breathing in the horror of the scene. Despite the innocence of her youthful features, she looked hungry for more carnage.

He'd seen that look before.

Even though her hands were clean, she was changing, already losing part of herself, minute by minute, and nothing he could do would change that.

He was wrong. He was so wrong about her.

"I want to see," she said, shoving past him before he could stop her.

His voice croaked as he tried to call her back, but speaking after a transformation was always difficult. He never should have helped her. He should have known by the way she looked, spoke, and acted.

He waited in shame, knowing that the body was mauled and distorted. The face frozen in shock with its mouth wide, the throat devoured so deep that the head was almost severed from the body.

When Red came back out, a grin stretched her pale pink lips.

The sight disturbed him so much he looked away and out into the welcome calm of the dark forest.

She was so much like Ana it made his gut twist.

29

OCLEAU

THE YEAR OF THE CURSE

BLAEZ

The sky softened as twilight crept in, but it brought only gray skies and droplets of rain. Keeping the hood of his cloak drawn over his head to shelter him, Blaez made the journey to the witch's house. Everyone whispered warnings to avoid her, yet all the townsfolk went to her in times of need. Ana was in dire need of saving, and he would deliver her a cure, no matter the cost. Money or his life, he would give it for her. No matter how many times she split his lip or threw something at him, he would pick up the pieces and make them fit again. Even if it left him scarred.

Along the gnarled path, worn down from countless desperate footsteps, a doe crossed before him. She stepped out from the slender trees, her black-tipped ears flickering. Nose raised high, she turned her head and stared at Blaez before disappearing into the trees on the other side of the path. A moment of serenity followed, bringing a sense of calmness that overtook Blaez. *I should leave this place*, he thought. Still, he carried on.

Stepping into the clearing, the house craned over him, and atop the highest peak perched a large crow with giant black eyes that bore right through him. A knot formed in his gut, though crows and ravens had never bothered him before. He saw many when hunting and he respected them for their cunning. Often, they would share a kill. When he was out in the woods, he ate mostly rabbit, though they offered little substance. Blaez would leave enough behind for whatever might come to pick the fleshy head clean and feast on the entrails.

Blaez knew the creature before him was no ordinary bird from the way it studied him. Whatever calm he'd felt from the presence of the doe quickly withered as discomfort took over.

Despite the eerie feeling and internal voices screaming at him to run, Blaez walked to the witch's door and knocked thrice. He only had to wait a few seconds before it opened, swinging inwards. Face to face with the same young woman he had gone to many years ago, Blaez welcomed the familiarity. Her captivating green eyes reminded him of the first grasses coming up from a hard winter.

"What brings you to our door?" she asked warmly, reaching for his hands. Her demeanor relaxed him.

"My wife is ill, and I'm afraid she does not have much time."

Something flashed in her eyes, but she quickly sidestepped so Blaez could enter the house; he suspected it was recognition until she shut the door behind him. "What is your name?"

"Blaez Kõiv," he told her without hesitation. "And you are Juniper; we have met before."

She cocked her head to the side, then nodded. "You have a good memory. That was many years ago."

"I am good with faces," he replied. Her very presence carried a sense of serenity, reminding him of the doe he saw earlier. Reminding him there was still good in this world.

Thankful that she didn't inquire whether or not Ana had become with child, Blaez offered her a soft smile. Sensing another presence in the room, he shifted his gaze over to where the figure stood. The woman was tall, hunched over at the top of her spine where it curved from age and the long years of bending over fires and books. The notorious witch of Ocleau, her name moving to the far reaches of the town—Azalea Luca.

"What ails her?" Azalea asked, stepping into the light of the lanterns and fire.

"She was bedridden when I returned home from a hunt, unable to eat—if she does manage, it does not stay down. Her fever burns, and she couldn't tell me how long she had been this way... I don't know what I would do without her..." Blaez's voice tapered off into a faded crackle.

"What would you do to save her?" Azalea asked, stepping up to him and matching his stature when she straightened herself. She was completely cold, a stark contrast to the warmth her daughter had shown him, without an ounce of sympathy on her face.

Blaez supposed that in her life, seeing what she saw every day, she had to be cold.

Blaez paused for only a moment before replying, "Anything."

Azalea seemed pleased with this answer, but she continued, "Would you die for her?"

"Yes." This time he did not hesitate. He withstood her beatings just to be allowed to lay beside her in bed, to look upon her and be content that she allowed him to love her. It pained him to know the cost, but if her well-being cost him his life, then he would give it. While he had considered leaving her, he refused to have her death on his conscience. If he had the opportunity to help her, he had to take it. He now wondered what he would be without Ana in his life, by his side. To die for her would be the last way to prove to her how much he loved her.

"I can cure her. You need not die for her." Azalea told him, snapping him out of his thoughts.

"I have very little money," he admitted. "I am not a man to beg, but I would fall on my knees and beg for her life. I would be forever indebted to you if that were what you wished. Tell me whatever you need, and you will have it."

She raised a sharp eyebrow, perhaps impressed and intrigued, perhaps disbelieving. He was not certain.

Then she nodded. "Yes, you will do."

"Me?" He looked at her in disbelief. "You want me?"

"Return three days from now in the late afternoon, an hour before the moon rises and before the sun has set."

He scrambled to focus on the instructions she gave him, repeating them in his head.

"If you are but a moment late," the witch continued, "your wife will succumb to her illness. If you turn back on this deal, your wife will die. If you so much as think—"

"Mama," Juniper warned her mother to stop. "He has shown his desperation to save her; do not push him so far that he will not show up."

Blaez looked at Juniper, trying to read her, then back to Azalea. "I will not be late."

"You better not be if you want your pretty little wife to live."

Blaez tilted his head forward and narrowed his eyes at her. "How do you know my wife is pretty?"

"I assume. A man like you would not settle for less," she said. She gestured to the door. "You may go now."

Blaez turned partway, then stopped and straightened out again. He shook his head and looked Azalea dead in the eyes. For a moment, a silence passed over the room, settling deep into the bones of the house, the foundation. "Something to ease her pain, at the very least."

Azalea opened her mouth to protest, but Juniper stepped in front of her mother. The moment of bitter tension between them was impossible to miss. Blaez could feel it, rippling through the air like hot and cold.

Juniper was firm when she spoke. "Of course—we will give you a temporary cure until you have upheld your end of the bargain. Once that is complete, we will hand over enough to fix her permanently."

Wordlessly, Azalea rummaged through her cabinets and brought them to a nearby table. She stirred and poured, strange smells and the sounds of herbs grinding filling the room. After a few moments, she turned and handed Blaez a leather pouch with a cork-stop in it. Liquid sloshed within it as Blaez took it, worried it might spill. Clutching it tight to his body, Blaez met Juniper's eyes and nodded his thanks. He did not do the same for Azalea, who remained prickly and irritable. *But Juniper is soft. Juniper is someone who can—like Ana—get anyone to do anything for them. Only she does not appear to abuse it quite like Ana.*

Azalea's voice interrupted him. "Have her drink a quarter of it tonight and another in the morning when the sun rises. Repeat in the evening, then in the morning after. There is only enough for two days, and on the third day, when you return, I promise you she will be safe. She will survive."

Although Blaez didn't like the sound of it, he nodded. He did not have a choice; his answer was always Ana, even if it killed him. He went to the door, feeling sweat prickle under his jacket in the warmth. At the door, with his hand on the knob and the frigid air greeting him like an old friend, he paused. Unsure what he wanted the answer to be, he asked, "In three days... Will I ever see Ana again?"

"Perhaps," Azalea replied.

30

SILVANIA

THE YEAR OF THE MOON

RED

Red stood above her grandmother's mangled form. She smiled as she knelt to touch the body; it was still warm. Blood pooled around her gaping wounds, her corpse no longer resembling anything human. *But Grandmother was never really human. All her actions were inhumane.* Red searched inside of herself, trying to find some feeling of sadness and remorse, but she found nothing. All she felt was gratitude toward the Wolf.

She'd peeked when he stepped out of his clothing and made the transformation. It left her in utter shock. A part of her didn't believe in the Wolf until she saw him, massive haunches covered in black fur blending into the shadows. Now that she knew the truth, Red wondered how much further she could go. Killing her father was next, but what if she went bigger? *Could I rule all of Silvania?* she wondered. *Could I make a difference?*

With Alina, Sorin, Tatiana, and Lilianna at her side and the Wolf at her heels, she could bring peace and order to the spiteful town. A yearning for power, and the desire to keep anyone from hurting another young woman again, raged inside her. Her first assailant was dead, her father would be next. *Then who? Mr. Floarea? Every other parent who laid a hand on their children?*

She rose from her crouched position, admiring the pulverized carcass of her grandmother once more. Navigating the house with tiptoe precision, as she was so accustomed to doing there, Red reached the front door in her own time. Her face lit up when she made it there, surprised at what faced her when she exited the musty building.

"Alina?"

Red was shocked to see the other girls standing outside, their bare feet digging into the dirt to feel the power of the Earth beneath them. Their hair was a mess, and Tatiana was covered in blood.

"Red!" Alina pushed to the front of the group. Halfway up the stairs to the porch, the two girls met in an embrace.

Red smelled lavender and blood in her hair. *Such a strange combination. The scent of something so soothing paired with something so volatile.*

"I thought I would never see you again," Alina said, holding Red's cheeks in her hands. "Are you alright?"

"Yes, I am." Red looked at the girls one by one. Then she asked, "What are you doing here?"

"We came to rescue you," Sorin said, scrutinizing the man on the porch, "but it appears you have things well under control."

Red broke away from Alina and glanced over at the man. "This is the Wolf."

Lilianna beamed up at him, then leaned to her sister and murmured, "He's very handsome."

Alina strode up to him, jabbing her finger into his chest. "What are your intentions? The stories we have heard about you are inconsistent at best, and from what I can see, you have not laid a hand on Red. What are you doing here?"

He opened his mouth to speak, then paused for a moment as though figuring out what to say.

Red spoke for him. "He helped me. My grandmother is finally

dead. She'll never lay her hand on me again. Go on inside, take a look."

No one needed to; they believed her.

Sorin glared up at the man, placing her hands on her voluptuous hips. "Our protection spell worked, then?"

"I'm not sure," Red admitted. "The curse took me, yes...but he," she pointed at the Wolf, "never lays a hand on any of the girls. In fact, he helps them. I know it didn't work because he said he would have transformed and killed whomever my father wanted dead immediately after I arrived. It brought me to him, but nothing more."

A silence filled the tense air around them; Sorin looked at the Wolf with distrust but softened as she considered Red's words. The truth surrounded them—Red was untouched, and her grandmother was dead. The other girls were all safe, too.

"I have to kill my father," Red continued. Feeling their eyes on her as they listened felt good. "I'll need your help, all of you. After that, I have much bigger plans. I will need each and every one of you by my side."

"What is it?" Lilianna asked, her eyes shining.

Red walked towards the Wolf and stood before him. "I will need your help. I understand that you do not wish to kill. I am sorry I ever asked it of you—from here on out, I will do better. I will take life with my own hands to gain what I seek." She turned towards the four young women. "With your help, I can take Silvania and make it better, make it safe for people like us. The abused, the molested, the hunted." She looked at the Wolf. "The cursed."

"Red, what are you suggesting?" Alina asked.

"We will kill my father. Then we find the scroll that controls him." She pointed at the Wolf. "We show the town that we have it, that we are more powerful than all of them. They will not try to string us up, burn us, or drive us out if we have him at our side. This town has been terrified of him for nearly four hundred years."

"I will not be your pet," the man snapped. "I have been *controlled* and *used* for centuries. I will not stand to be controlled by a group of girls—especially witches. I have had enough dealings with witches for my lifetime."

"Listen to me," Red said sternly. "We will never, ever use you for the curse; we have no daughters to sacrifice. With the scroll—which I am sure is in my home—the townsfolk will not dare undermine us. We do not have to use you for power. We will ensure that the curse never gets used again—and I promise we will one day find a way to sever your connection to it."

He stared at Red as if wanting to believe her words. But whatever he saw in her eyes struck him with terror. He shook his head. "It will not work. Nothing can undo the curse."

Sorin cut in. "I may know a way. The curse is powerful, yes, but I think it is quite simple. Old magic. You help us, and I will do everything in my power to help you."

He looked desperate, clawing at any chance to be free. His head dropped. "I swore never to trust a witch again."

"We have changed," Sorin promised him.

"Give me your word," he said after a moment of labored silence.

"I promise," Sorin said.

"I promise," Alina repeated.

Lilianna and Tatiana spoke simultaneously, pinkies interlacing as they said, "We promise."

Red smiled. "I promise."

31

OCLEAU

THE YEAR OF THE CURSE

JUNIPER

"Will you walk with me in the woods?" Azalea asked two hours before moonrise.

Juniper looked up at her mother. "Of course, Mama."

The sky faded to a white-gray that reminded her of ash. It was going to snow. The route they took had no path—just the woods, unmolested by men. A pure place. They did not need to go far before Azalea stopped. "Here is good."

"What happens here?" Juniper inquired quietly.

Azalea's arm was still tightly entwined with Juniper's when she turned to face her. With her free hand, Azalea slipped out a scroll and unrolled it. The parchment shook in the soft wind.

Juniper's heart sank. She didn't feel fear, nor anger, just sadness. She knew what her mother was going to do. *My life is not hers to take*, she thought sourly.

She pulled free of her mother and stared her down. "What happens here?" she repeated.

The dull gray evening faded to black; soon, the full moon would be in effect. Juniper foolishly thought her mother had found nothing that would ensure her control over the man—the Wolf. It appeared that it was nothing that Juniper was privy to. The look Azalea gave her now suggested otherwise. She did not tell Juniper because she was part of the answer. The cold from the rock-hard ground seeped through her shoes, but it was nothing compared to the chill she felt from the look on her mother's face.

Juniper didn't complain; it simply wasn't in her nature. In a slender, naked tree behind her mother sat the crow. Juniper knew what the familiar was capable of doing to a person. She knew that if she ran, she would be torn apart until she was forced to submit.

"Why did you bring me out here, Mama?" She watched her mother's face carefully. *She knows I warned Matthias, that I begged him to leave before it was too late.*

She shook her head. Was that really something that could be viewed as betrayal? In her heart, she knew the answer was yes. If there was one thing she learned over the years about her mother, it was that she could not be trusted, even at the best of times. Juniper understood this a long time ago when she killed Riina. All Azalea spoke of for ten years was Matthias's return. How she wished he would come back. She wanted him back because he would carry on the family name. He was the son of the only man she ever loved.

It was something Juniper couldn't do. *I was safe so long as it was just us, for Mama would never push away both her children.* But Azalea's favorite was back, the one that could protect her, take care of her, and give her proper grandchildren with a woman of her choosing. *Matthias will never do that for her. Especially if I do not make it out of this forest alive.*

Juniper knew Matthias only agreed to stay for her. Earlier, he had asked for the cure for Ana, begging Juniper to make him something. That's when she knew Matthias had something planned, and she could only hope he would not screw it up. To hide something from Azalea was a difficult—but doable—task.

"Mama, please answer me."

Azalea reached her hand up and placed it against Juniper's cheek. "You were always the sweetest of my children."

"That is very kind of you to say," Juniper said. "Mama, why are we here and not preparing for the displacement?"

"We are, my child," Azalea replied. She placed a blank scroll on the ground and set rocks on each corner to keep it unrolled. Then she reached into her pocket and withdrew a crumpled piece of paper, clearly torn from an old book.

"What do you need from me?" Juniper asked, though she did not want to know. Up in the tree, Aegidius hopped along the branches, growing closer in case Juniper fled.

"You are the most important ingredient, Juniper." Her mother's eyes burned. "The agony I must bear will give me full control of the Wolf, and everyone who uses the curse after me will have to suffer the same agony I will tonight."

"What agony?" Juniper stepped back from her mother's touch, just beyond her reach.

"The most powerful of curses require a blood sacrifice, Juniper. You will be mine."

Juniper shrank back as Azalea pulled a knife from her pocket. She brandished it before her, staring at Juniper as a twisted grin stretched across her face.

Juniper knew that Azalea's smile was authentic, the smile of a mother who loves her son beyond sanity, more than she could ever love her daughter. Jealousy tore at Juniper's heart, quickly turning to disgust. Disgust that she ever followed her mother down this path, wishing she had run away with Matthias all those years ago. But she had been corrupted, her mother whispering things in her ear since birth, making her choose her over common sense.

"Matthias was right to leave," Juniper cried in fury, though she trembled where she stood. "Do you think he will stay here with you when he finds out you've murdered me?"

"You are so naïve, child. Either he will be my Wolf, or he will be kept here by one. A blood oath will keep him here regardless of what he is. When he kills that succubus who has latched onto him, he will have nothing left. And because you betrayed me, planting the seed of escape in his head, his daughter will have to die, too. The curse I will create tonight will cost us both our daughters."

"That is what pushed him away in the first place, you pitiless crone," Juniper spat.

Azalea simply smiled. "A broken man can only be comforted by his mother. In time, he will accept this. He will not be allowed to leave this town without my permission. Now, that is enough talking, child. On your knees."

Juniper considered running—she was much faster than her mother. Even if her mother's familiar didn't catch up to her, the thought of running through the bitter cold to greet nothing but locked doors chilled her to the bone. She knew no one would let a witch into their home. She had dug her own grave the moment she began working with Azalea. *I hope Matthias is smarter than Azalea believes him to be.*

Juniper dropped to her knees, slamming hard into the ground. Juniper's placid features fell, lips curling down as tears lined her eyes. She looked up at her mother, keeping her hands loose by her side. Her hair hung freely over her shoulders, the mousy brown strands resembling the tree bark around her.

The forest was once her sanctuary.

A beautiful doe stepped into sight, and Juniper made eye contact with her familiar. She shook her head slowly to tell her to stay where she was. Either way, the doe would die. If she interfered with Azalea's plan, her mother would slaughter the deer and eat her for supper once she finished with Juniper. If she stood aside, she would die when Juniper did as the link between their souls severed.

"Matthias will find out what you have done here," Juniper repeated as Azalea unsheathed the silver blade. "He will make sure you are brought to justice."

"Enough, child." Azalea kissed Juniper upon each cheek, then her forehead, before moving behind her.

How many times has she kissed me like that? Juniper thought helplessly. *I wish her love for me had been real.*

"You never could love me as much as him. But he *never* loved you, Mama. I did." Juniper sobbed. "You could n-never love a child of rape. But it wasn't my fault."

"I know, Juniper. But you are wrong about one thing," Azalea replied, placing the blade against her throat.

Juniper choked back another sob, the dagger digging into her flesh with the movement of her throat. It instantly drew blood, the blade horrifically sharp. But it did not hurt.

"I always loved you. You were proof that good could come out of so much evil."

Juniper laughed sourly. "You let my existence justify all the evil you've done? That makes you no better than my father."

"He was not your father," Azalea snapped. "You have no father. Just a mother."

"You are my mother no more." Juniper lifted her head to the skies, watching as the clouds shifted and broke slightly. She saw the molasses sky and hoped the moon would never rise. For her, it would be darkness forever.

Azalea whispered something in a language Juniper did not recognize, her voice starting as a low growl and gradually increasing in volume. A throaty rumble echoed from deep in her chest. The words filled the forest around them, and in between the trees, Juniper watched as her doe dipped her head, then folded her legs underneath her.

With her head on the dirt, they locked eyes as Azalea gripped the knife a little tighter in sweating palms, pulling it to the side swiftly.

As the doe let out her dying breath on the forest floor, words formed on the scroll before Azalea. Blood seeped into the ground to the roots of the trees and appeared on the parchment as ink.

Juniper's body twitched twice before she saw nothing but darkness.

Azalea

Juniper

Matthias — Rum

Elva

PART IV
The Coven

32

SILVANIA

THE YEAR OF THE MOON

RED

Inside the house, surrounded by the scent of blood and decay, Red developed her plan. With the presence of the other women at her side, she felt protected and empowered. Love for them bloomed inside her, taking hold and growing at an uncontrollable rate. They had all come to her aid when only weeks ago, her disappearance would have gone completely unnoticed. A swell of gratitude filled her, overwhelming her. She swam through her newfound emotions as she tried to focus on what had to be done.

"Sorin, Alina, can you do it? Can you sever him from his curse?" Red asked.

Sorin looked around the house, her hands touching the books and scrolls that lined the shelves. Trinkets that were a shadow of the family history sat covered in dust. A handheld mirror, candles with their wax dripping like permanent icicles, an intricate candle stuffer. Sorin stepped back and pushed a stray curl out of her face. Her black hair had grown tangled, her shapely figure revealed by her thin night dress.

The room grew quiet as they waited for an answer. A stale feeling, pregnant with dread, hung in the air.

Sorin glanced over her shoulder. "I believe I can, but I will need you, Red."

"Me?" Red asked. "Why me?"

"I will explain later."

"Very well," Red agreed, trusting in whatever Sorin had planned. She looked at Tatiana and Lilianna. "I need you both to bring my father here."

"To kill him?" Lilianna asked with a grin, newfound bloodlust in her eyes now that her father was deceased.

Tatiana shot her a wide-eyed glance, making the whites of her eyes brighter through her blood-stained face. She pursed her lips together as though she wanted to chide her sister but held back.

"Yes," Red said. "We cannot be free with our oppressors still alive and breathing down our necks. Tatiana, you must wear my cloak and make him follow you. But keep your distance. He will think I am dead because of the sacrifice; he will follow you to see what went wrong. Lilianna, you must break into my house and retrieve the scroll. It will be in the den, the room on the eastern side of the house, facing the fields. Once my father follows Tatiana, you'll be able to sneak in. My mother never steps foot in the den, but make sure to be quiet."

They nodded at the same time as though they were one. Sisters who had endured so much of the same pain, with only each other to hold and protect...to suffer with.

Red pulled her cloak off and handed it to Tatiana.

Red glanced at the older two again. "We do not sever the curse until my father is dead. As a precautionary measure."

The Wolf looked at her, his black eyes narrowed into slits.

Red knew the change in her was frightening, it made her shiver deep inside, but it had waited dormant for too long. She'd always felt something inside of her simmering below the surface. *And now I will release it from its cage.*

The Wolf had nothing to worry about; none of them had daughters to sacrifice. *And yet, I have already made him kill someone.*

Ignoring his glare, Red turned back to Tatiana and Lilianna. "Go. Be back before sunrise."

They nodded and disappeared out the front door. No one had tended to the fire, and a chill crept into the house that then refused to leave. She wondered how Sorin planned to use her to undo the curse. Nervous but refusing to show it, she looked at the two witches flipping through books and scrolls.

"They have no idea what they are doing," the Wolf snarled accusingly. "They are children, you are all children—I have put my fate into the hands of foolish young girls who think witchcraft will save them. It will not save you; it will be the death of you. I have seen hundreds of witches burned alive, half of whom were innocent women accused blindly. I do not wish to see the five of you suffer the same. Witchcraft is poison."

Red was growing tired of his disdain. With venom in her voice, she hissed, "Witchcraft saved my life. Have a little faith, and it may save yours."

He growled, but Alina cut in. "What choice do you have? What do you have to lose by trying?" She marched up to him and jabbed her finger into his chest again. "We have everything to lose by helping you. "

"This will not end the way you wish it to." He turned his back on them, disappearing into the other room.

"Go after him," Alina told Red. "We will continue here."

Red left to ensure the Wolf wasn't about to run. She found him seated on the bottom of the porch steps.

His filthy bare feet were planted firmly on the dirt. His hands were clasped in his lap, fingers unmoving. A gentle gust of wind blew his messy hair, but he did not appear to notice. No goosebumps prickled along his arms, though Red found herself chilled without her red cloak.

"Tell me more about Ana," Red said.

"I don't want to talk about her."

"Is there anything you do wish to discuss?" Red implored. "I do not know your name—though it appears that neither do you. Perhaps if you talked about what you do remember, you might recall more of your past."

"What makes you think I wish to remember anything? I remember every single family I slaughtered, I remember every single girl that came to me as you did, I remember every detail of every murder except hers." His voice broke slightly. "I just remember waking up with blood on my hands, her corpse so mauled I could hardly make out her face."

He sighed deeply, as though speaking about it was slowly revealing his guilt to the world. Red wanted to wrap her hands around that guilt and take it away from him if it would mean he would open up to her. *I want to know more, about him, about Ana, about how he came to be. He is the last person alive from when it happened. What a burden that must be.*

"It snowed that day. I remember it being fiercely cold. I remember...sickness. She was sick." He glanced at his hands, caked with dirt. His brows pulled tight, pain etching into his downturned mouth. "It does not matter how I recall it anymore; the outcome is always the same. Her blood on my hands, on my tongue, dripping from my hair, my naked body... They strung me up after. They were going to kill me—and I still wish they had."

"Could they have killed you?" Red asked. "You have lived this long; surely nothing can."

"I have tried many times. Over the years, I learned only one thing can kill me; one hundred years of starvation." He glanced forlornly out at the forest. The sun was going to make its appearance soon, and the moon would take her leave. "I tried to do it, you know. To starve myself. I wasn't strong enough."

Red softened, his words melting her angry resolve. "I am sorry this has happened to you. If anyone can separate you from the curse, it is Sorin." Red hoped that he would believe her words as she did. "I won't...I won't use you for power. It is not right to ask that of you when it is all that has been asked of you for so long. Once we sever the curse, you're free to go. Choose life, choose death, choose to stand by our sides—the choice is yours. Can you forgive me for what I made you do?"

He looked at her, confusion in his eyes.

Red truly did want his forgiveness but knew she would use any means possible to change Silvania. *The Wolf doesn't need to be privy to that, though*, she thought.

"Yes," he answered. "I forgive you."

She smiled, flooded by a rush of warmth at the thought that things would be different from now on.

A red cloak appeared as Tatianna came through the forest shadows with Lilianna close behind, clutching the scroll in her hands.

"He's coming," Tatiana said.

33

OCLEAU

THE YEAR OF THE CURSE

BLAEZ

On the morning that would change his fate, Blaez woke with stiff bones and an unshakable chill. Having fallen asleep in the living room chair with nothing but fur draped over him, he had allowed the fire to die while he slept. An ominous feeling settled over him, and he rose with creaking joints and a stiff neck.

He stretched, then rebuilt the fire, preparing for his daily chores. He milked the cows, then prepared a generous bath when he returned. He used the blazing fire to heat the water, pouring the near-scalding water over himself to cleanse away the sickness and worry. The hours moved slowly, like molasses, and he checked in on Ana as he counted down the time until he would save her. Outside in the bitter cold, the clouds promised snow. The forests stood calm and unmoving. *I might never see her again*, he thought. But it was something he could live with. His deal with the witch was his solution; he could escape Ana's abuse without leaving her.

He wondered what she would do without him. He wondered what his life would be like after tonight. *Best not to dwell too much*, he thought. But he had very little to distract himself with. He knew he did not have to do it, that he could allow her to drift away and die. It would be the right thing for *him*, letting her illness take its course and finally being free. But Blaez knew it was not the moral thing to do, not if he could help her; doing what was morally right was more important than doing the right thing for himself.

Ana's spirits had improved since he gave her the tonic. Though she still remained bedridden, she was able to keep food down, and color slowly crept back to her cheeks. As she thrived, Blaez came to terms with his choice to sacrifice whatever he had to in order to keep her alive.

Freshly bathed, he stepped outside, goosebumps prickling his exposed forearms. He looked at the setting sun and sighed. The moon rose, full.

All the dread and anticipation Blaez had been building hit him at once, creating an anxious knot in the pit of his stomach. He stepped back inside, threw another log on the fire, then dug for the parchment he bought the day before. *It was costly, but some things are worth the price.* With a quill and a scant amount of ink, Blaez sat down and began to write.

Dearest Ana,

It is with a heavy heart that I pen this letter. I know these may very well be the last words from me to you. To say them to you in person would have been ideal, but I have never been a man of many words. To convey them properly to someone as important as you, they must be put to paper. Please know there is no part of me that wishes to leave you. I won't reminisce about our time together, because there was less good than either of us is willing to admit.

I made a deal with a witch to keep you alive; your life means more to me than my own, and it always has. I suspect I will not come out of this unscathed. The man that I am is the one you know, and so you must understand I would do anything to keep you safe. My trust in this witch is limited, but I do believe she will uphold her end of the deal. Should she not, I am truly sorry, and I will continue to find every way possible to save you.

Our life has never been an easy one. I know you never loved me. This is why I know I must get you through this, even if I do not—you deserve love, and I have already found it. It is you who gets us through; whenever I gaze upon your face and imagine my life without you, I am terrified. Once this is done, I will not see you again; I knew that before I agreed to whatever comes next. I can live a life without you if I know that you are safe.

I know I have not made you happy or met your needs. Though I always strive to find everything you need and give it to you regardless of its cost to me, this is the last testament of my love for you. To stay away from you will be hard, but knowing it will keep you safe will provide me with some solace. A long time ago, you wished for a child that I could not give you; if it was my indifference to children that made you store the herbs *in the depths of a drawer to never look at again, I am truly sorry that I failed you.*

Maybe when I am gone, you will find peace.
I truly hope you do.
BlaeZ.

So much of it was a lie, but their whole relationship together had been one. A façade to outsiders. Married for convenience but learned to love each other. Blaez shook his head. He didn't think Ana knew how to love. *Sometimes lying makes us better people. I hope this letter is enough.*

Blaez folded the paper into thirds and scrawled *Ana* on it. Knowing he had to depart shortly, Blaez took one last look around the house, not daring to enter the bedroom, knowing that looking at Ana one last time would make it too difficult to leave.

Donning his hunting jacket, Blaez left the house and his marriage behind him. As he began to put distance between himself and his old life, he allowed himself to go numb. *Just move your feet; left, right, left, right.* The frozen dirt crunched loudly beneath each footfall as he walked.

He passed through the town, eyes averted. There were only a few faces out and about in the last hours of twilight, but not one greeted him as he passed.

Blaez reached the edge of the forest and pressed on before his legs failed him, stepping carefully around the roots and fallen branches. The last light of day could not penetrate the canopy above, plunging the woods into thick darkness. He embraced it, allowing it to overtake him. He felt safe for a few moments as if he were just on another hunt. His anxious thoughts disappeared, his only focus getting to the eerie house deep in the woods.

This time, there was no doe. No beautiful creature crossed his path to let him know everything would be alright.

All too soon, the house stood before him. The massive, lurking crow atop the peak glared down at him; he refused to meet its black eyes, walking up the creaking stair and knocking on the door that led to his fate.

His blood screamed not to do it.

34

SILVANIA

THE YEAR OF THE MOON

THE WOLF

He entered the house again. A fire burned in the hearth now, the quiet crackle of wood giving the illusion of cozy warmth. But no one felt it. Instead, a cold, sinister dread enveloped the room in its long arms, coaxing out the deepest hatred.

Two young women knelt on a floor covered in salt, dirt, and candles with flames like tiny orange dancers. Among the scattered remnants of the Craft was distinguishable blood; he could smell it. His taste buds recalled the flavor of it; it belonged to the grandmother.

"What is all this?" he asked.

The blonde looked up. "We think the spell cast upon you four hundred years ago requires direct blood from the family to remove it. Sorin and I are trying something we have never done before."

"How comforting," he replied sarcastically. *Trusting witches never did me any good.* Gears began to turn in his head. *Does that mean Red is a Luca?* He walked behind the witches to study the tapestry that clung to the wall. He gripped the dusty fabric as he examined it, parts of it moth-eaten and crumbling in his grip. Her words spun over and over as he pulled the tapestry from the wall with a hard yank.

The action revealed a massive family tree painted across the wood.

It was a beautiful piece of art painted by a skillful hand. He grabbed a candle from the ground, ignoring Sorin's protest, and brought it to the tree to read the words inscribed near each branch. At the bottom was Rose Luca, and directly above her were Victor Luca and Maria Popova. Above that was the name Heather, with all four of her siblings labeled deceased, including their mother.

They all died on the same day, he realized.

Though he wanted to look at the top of the tree, fearing what he would find but desperate to know, he looked at every name. His eyes found a name that had been scratched out, burned, and blackened—all that was legible was 'Toren.' A few branches over another name had been crossed out, though sloppily, it was clear enough to read 'Mihai.' Nearly all of them were labeled as deceased; many did not have children. There was barely anyone left living from this family. He looked up and up, tracing each name with his fingers until he reached the top of the tree.

At the top sat Azalea Luca.

What he saw just below Azalea's name left him in shock; he stumbled back, stepping on someone's foot. His name came barreling back to him, slamming into his consciousness.

A yelp brought him back to his senses and surroundings, and he looked to see that he had bumped into Red, who looked so much like…

"What…" he stammered, his head shaking side to side slightly. He gripped his head with one hand, the other leaning against the wall for support. He no longer trusted his legs to keep him upright. "What did you say about the family blood?"

"We need blood from the Luca family to stop your curse—soon, we will have three generations of their blood here, and then we can proceed to attempt this removal," Alina explained, glancing at Sorin to confirm what she was saying. "Once Red's father arrives, we will add his blood to the circle. Then Red will offer some of her blood willingly, just as you once gave your life willingly."

"You know this for certain?" he asked.

Alina nodded. "I've studied the lore, myths, and legends. To break a curse requires willingness. And to fully reverse this curse, Red must sacrifice her father."

"The daughter has to sacrifice the father, turning the curse in on itself," Sorin explained.

"So, she..." He turned to look at Red.

"Is a descendant of the witch that cursed you, yes."

He looked back at the family tree, the name staring at him. He shook all over, cold sweat dripping down his muscular back. It all came rushing back to him—Ana's sickness, the witch, the curse being transferred to him, the blood on his hands.

No, it didn't make sense...

The ghost of his past tapped his arm. Her eyes bore into him as she asked, "Are you alright?"

Nausea churned in his stomach; he was certainly not alright, but he forced a nod.

Red offered him a smile. "My father is going to be here any minute. We need your help."

"I never thought I would be helping a Luca," he muttered under his breath.

"Not all of us are like her," she told him. "I had a great aunt who was driven out of the town, though there is some debate over whether she was evil; it depends on who you ask. There are other members of the family who have been cast out over the years. I suppose some of us get less Luca blood than the others."

He looked at her, studying the face that looked so much like Ana's. Withholding a cringe at an evil thought that wormed through his brain, he had to look away from Red—Rose Luca—in order to keep his thoughts contained. He glanced once more at the family tree, then back at Red.

"Not all of us are our parents, grandparents, or ancestors," Red added.

"You're right," he admitted as four centuries of loathing began to fade.

"He's here," Tatiana said. She had been peeking through the curtains, quickly replacing them as she withdrew. The young women gravitated toward the center of the room, surrounding him. Circling as though they were protecting him.

Red whispered, "I won't ask you to do anything…but if things do not go as planned…"

"I will help you," he told Red. "The death of a power-hungry Luca will not stain my conscience."

Heavy footsteps came up the groaning, crooked stairs. A gentle knock followed, and when no reply came from within, the door creaked open. Dawn broke, the gentle morning rays coming through the door when it opened. The moment Victor—Red's father—stepped into the house, it was clear from the disgusted look on his face that he sensed something was wrong.

"Mother?" he asked, his voice hoarse. The voice of a tired man.

His eyes adjusted to the candle-lit room as he focused on four young women—his daughter among them—and a stranger. His eyes narrowed. A look of pure murder crossed Victor's expression, and the Wolf realized he had seen that look on many of the Lucas before him. *Red was right about some children inheriting the Luca gene more than others,* he thought as he protectively stepped in front of the young women. They would not be harmed by this monster; no more blood would be shed by a Luca's hand.

35

OCLEAU

THE YEAR OF THE CURSE

AZALEA

Azalea stumbled weakly back to the house, barely holding the bowl of cedar, borage, and scabiosa steady.

Juniper's fresh, warm blood darkened the shavings.

The drink which Matthias and Blaez would both consume sat in a cauldron over the fire, thickening. Azalea grabbed two chalices and filled them with slow, calculated scoops of the ladle. The blackening brew smelled horrific, but she did not turn away from the scent. Ensuring an hour had passed since Juniper's sacrifice, she poured the mixture into the cup she would feed to Blaez. An ache spread through her chest, but she had no time to give in to the emotion. The front door opened, and Matthias entered the house.

He turned to his mother, his gray eyes ablaze. Black circles were evident under his eyes as though he had smeared the charcoal at the bottom of the roaring flames beneath them. His skin had become sallow, the toll of the curse obvious on him as the full moon neared.

Azalea imagined the fear that swept over him the last few days, worrying what would happen if she failed. Recalling the terror when he shifted last time. From a man to a deadly Wolf, he would lose control again.

"You look dreadful," Azalea told him outright.

"Of course, I do," he growled back at her. "If you fail, who dies? You? Ana? Juniper? Me?"

Azalea flinched when he mentioned Juniper. "Yes."

A grimace made him look even worse off. "Do you care?"

"Yes," she repeated. Meeting his gaze, Azalea told him confidently, "I will not fail."

His lips tightened into a thin, white line, his brows coming together in the center. "No one but him gets hurt."

Azalea knew he was referring to Blaez; he was only going to be hurt when he realized what he had done to his wife. He believed her to be so innocent, but she knew better. Sometimes being so close to someone blinded you to who they really were. Blaez and Matthias were both blind to what Ana truly was. Azalea knew the moment Blaez showed up that he had never laid a hand on Ana. She did wonder what the other woman's game was and what she had planned for Matthias, though none of it mattered. Ana would be dead by morning.

"After all I have done, you still do not trust me?" Azalea asked her son.

"I will never trust you," he snapped. He then loosened his shoulders. "I have no choice but to rely on you."

Aegidius's chilling caw bounced off the walls, startling them both.

Blaez had arrived.

His fist struck the wooden door, each knock desperate, as though the energy had been sapped from him.

He promised that he was willing to die for Ana, but Azalea wondered if he would be so eager to accept his fate if he knew what was to come. She wondered if he would still go through with it if he knew she was a liar. Though tempted to reveal it to Blaez to see his reaction, she knew it would only bring more suffering to her son.

"You do not need to trust me, but you're right—you do need me," Azalea said. She glanced at the front door and beckoned Matthias to open it. She welcomed the disruption to prevent Matthias from digging deeper. *He's blinded by love and how quickly he falls.*

Was Matthias not so clearly in love with the woman, Azalea might have spared her. But Ana was not a woman that could be trusted, and she refused to allow her to live when so many variables were present. It would be too easy for Ana to turn around and point her finger at Azalea. She had to die, or Matthias would leave with her the moment he got the chance. He had his replacement for his dead lover, and he'd located his child; he would flee, and Azalea could not allow that. Now, more than ever, she had to ensure that the Luca line continued.

Azalea's only hope to survive this would be to put the full blame on Blaez, saying that he lost control as a wolf. The evidence would show that he was to blame for Juniper and Ana's death. Though he had not killed Juniper, Azalea took extra steps to prepare her body as if a wolf had mauled her. He would be put on trial, but they could not kill Blaez once he was bound to the second curse, the one that would control him. The only way to break the curse was a hundred years of starvation; since this was impossible, he would never die.

After the town realizes they cannot kill this Wolf-man, after they learn that I'm in control of him, they will cower in fear, and I will run this town, she thought happily. *They did not need to know it cost me a daughter.*

Matthias tensed as he opened the door to allow Blaez to enter, glaring at the newcomer; Azalea knew with absolute certainty that her son was in love with this man's wife. There was no other reason for his obvious disdain.

"How is your wife?" Matthias asked. "Any improvement?"

"If there was, would I be here?" Blaez sounded exhausted.

"You are a kind husband." Matthias nodded. "I'm Matthias, Azalea's son."

Azalea focused on Blaez and took a deep breath. "What I am about to tell you may frighten you, but understand that the only way your wife will live through the night is if you listen and adhere to everything I tell you."

Blaez's features tightened, but he nodded.

"My son is cursed. He bears the curse of the full moon." Her eyes flitted between the men. Matthias's dark eyes were locked on Blaez, but Blaez looked at Azalea politely.

"You seem a strong man, both in body and mind."

Blaez only grunted in response.

"My son cannot handle the curse; he will not survive it," she half-lied. "But I can tell that you, Blaez, are capable of carrying this curse upon your back without much trouble—

"What happens on the full moon?"

Azalea had been dreading that question but suspected Blaez already knew the answer. "You become a creature. A wolf."

She could see the man try to wrap his mind around what she told him, his hands balling into fists and flexing repeatedly. As he considered her words, Azalea wondered if perhaps telling him had been a mistake but knew she had no choice; successful spellwork of this type required willingness.

After a moment of thought, Blaez let out a breath. "Very well."

Matthias gasped. "You will still go through with it?"

"For Ana," he said, looking Matthias dead in the eye, "I would do anything."

"Let us get this over with, then," Azalea cut in.

She grabbed the chalices, knowing exactly which one was for Blaez and which one was for Matthias. Blaez's was a slightly different color because it already contained Juniper's blood—the start of the curse she was setting into motion. Both men were unaware of such, and without knowledge of the Craft, neither could see the color difference in the lighting. Each man took their chalice, both looking skeptical, but Blaez held his head high. She respected him for that.

She walked over to Matthias and grabbed the knife she had used to slit Juniper's throat only hours before. Cleaned and sharpened, it would not even cause pain immediately. The blood would bead crimson and bright before Matthias felt a thing.

When Azalea sliced open the flesh upon Matthias's hand, he did not wince. The blood pooled immediately, but he remained stone still, trying to match Blaez's calmness. She flipped Matthias's hand and squeezed his fingers over the wound so his blood would spill. Then she held it over Blaez's cup, letting her son's blood drip into the potion. When it had filled almost to a spilling point, she pulled Matthias's hand back. He let it dangle at his side, the blood staining her floors.

Azalea took a deep breath and began to chant in the ancient tongue of the displacement curse. She felt the power coursing through her, and soon the words flowed from her lips as though it was her native language. They seized and silenced the room.

The two men stared at one another, Blaez's green gaze holding Matthias's gray, and they drank as though sealing a business deal. Matthias was the first to finish, and he dropped the chalice. Though it clattered upon the blood-stained floor, it did not distract Azalea. Her chanting persisted, and Matthias gasped as the air was suddenly pulled from his lungs.

Dark vapor came with it, billowing from him like smoke. His skin shriveled, and his veins turned black as Azalea spoke louder, ripping the curse from the depths of his body. His face twisted in pain, and, no longer able to contain it, he released a guttural scream.

The murky vapor gathered in a cloud above him, and Blaez stared wide-eyed as it wafted his way. Still, he showed no fear, not even when the smoke entered his mouth, searching for a new host. The color in his eyes faded, his veins blackening as the curse transferred to him. Consumed him.

When it was over, Blaez fell to his knees.

Azalea ceased chanting, waiting to see if the spell had worked. Blaez's head dropped, his hands hanging in front of him, shaking violently. Matthias had fallen on one knee, his hand gripping the edge of a table to keep himself upright.

It was Blaez who rose first, a distracted look in his once-determined eyes. Now a dull and listless gray, they gave him the appearance of something from nightmares, a dismal colorless dream.

He looked at Azalea, and for the first time, she was struck by his handsomeness. With a broken voice, he demanded, "The cure."

Surprised he was even able to speak, Azalea fetched the cure she had made the day Ana had arrived. She handed it to Blaez. Their hands touched briefly, and Blaez nodded his farewell. As he tried to step toward the door, eager to save his wife, he stumbled badly enough that he fell. Determined, he pulled himself back to his feet. As he staggered to the door, slowly regaining his ability to walk, Azalea handed Matthias a cup of tea to ease his pain.

Matthias managed to sit on a chair, finishing his tea as Blaez disappeared. "Thank you," he said, his voice fading.

Azalea watched his eyelids grow heavy and plucked the cup from his hand before it toppled. Matthias's head lolled back as the sleeping tonic took hold.

It is for the best, she thought. *I have work to do.*

36

SILVANIA

THE YEAR OF THE MOON

RED

Red watched her father assess the situation before him, scanning the room. A twitch in his nose suggested he noticed the stench of death. His hands clenched at his sides, quickly piecing together what had happened. Though his mother's corpse was nowhere in sight, the blood smeared over the floor in symbols could be from no one else. It was clear from his narrowing eyes he presumed the worst, though his glare could not penetrate the confidence of the six people before him.

"Father." Red stood calmly in front of the group. She took a threatening step toward him.

"You lasted longer than I thought you would." Victor's eyes narrowed. In the dim house, they looked almost black, matching the circles beneath his eyes. He glanced over the faces of the young women before him. "Thanks to your new friends, no doubt."

The women exchanged glances. No one was afraid of Victor. None of them showed an ounce of fear.

"Mr. Floarea won't be pleased when he hears where his daughters have been." He glowered at Tatiana and Lilianna. "And we all know what he does to his disobedient daughters."

"Our father is dead," Tatiana retorted.

Lilianna smirked. "We took matters into our own hands."

"Just as I will." Red cocked her head to the side, her eyes focused on her father.

"Do you really believe that a handful of girls who *think* they are witches can stop me?" Victor laughed.

"That's why we brought him, though I am happy to do this without his help. After all, you made me this way, Father." Red glanced at the Wolf standing to her right. He didn't move, as still as a marble statue. But the look in his eyes penetrated the distance between him and Victor, years of hatred for the Luca family buried deep in his bone marrow. It was clear he no longer felt guilt for what he may have to do.

"One man?" Victor asked though Red heard his voice wavering with fear.

"I think you know exactly who he is," Red pressed, enjoying his reaction.

Victor scoffed, desperately trying to grasp the upper hand and keep it.

"He has already murdered your mother," Red told him, hands clasping together in front of her hips. "I asked him to kill her, and then I asked him to help me kill you."

"Then what, Rose?" Victor snapped. "You return to a town that will bring you down the first chance they can? They will burn you on a pyre. It's what you deserve for your insolence, all of you. They will be reminded of the power of the curse. And you," he pointed at the Wolf, "will be used again and again until you are blinded by blood lust."

"We are removing the curse from him." Sorin stepped forward. "Lilianna, the scroll." She turned to the Wolf. "Get him on his knees."

The Wolf stepped forward, his feet padding silently across the floor as he approached Victor. Her father tried to step back, but the Wolf was faster, snatching a blade from the table before pulling the man into his arms and pressing the sharp blade to his throat.

Victor struggled, jerking himself out of the Wolf's grip. Pleased with himself for breaking free, Victor rose to his feet in defiance. He grinned, confident he was the bigger threat. Red smiled, knowing he wasn't.

Victor lunged.

Without hesitation, the Wolf snatched Victor's raised fist, gripping it so tightly that he cried out. The Wolf twisted his arm around his back, then kicked the back of his knees so he was forced to the floor.

Victor turned red with anger as he was shoved inside the center of the circle. He looked around, realizing he was surrounded by dirt and bones—both human and animal—and his mother's blood. It seeped from a severed, wrinkled finger with a large ring still upon it. Terror chiseled his features into a mask of horror. His head reared, desperate to get away from the carnage surrounding him. The Wolf gripped his collar to hold him in place, his feet firmly placed against Victor's back.

Alina took the scroll from Lilianna, who vibrated with excitement and handed it to Sorin.

She carefully spread it out, placing rocks on its curling edges. Red watched her scan the words, her tongue darting out between her lips as she focused. She nodded her head to her own thoughts every few moments, then at last, she looked up. Her eyes landed on Alina, who stood beside her, awaiting instruction.

"*'Hatred consumes,'*" Sorin read aloud. "*Feed this craving once and for all, end the reasoning for my enmity. End the blood that drips from the family, end their reign. I sacrifice my living, breathing daughter; yours to take as you will. Take that which I love to end that which I hate.'*" Sorin scoffed. "I wonder, can you truly love a child if you will sacrifice her? I do not believe you ever loved Red."

Victor snapped his head up to glare at Sorin, then winced as the blade bit into his stubble-covered neck. Blood beaded from the shallow wound.

"Perhaps that is why it did not work," Tatiana suggested.

"Perhaps," Sorin replied. She met Red's eyes. "Are you ready?"

Red stepped towards the circle without hesitation.

Keeping her father immobilized, the Wolf handed her the blade.

Her hands were steady as she took it, calmed by the strength of her Coven and the Wolf.

"You won't do it." Victor spat at his daughter, looking up from where he knelt at her feet.

Red spoke calmly, though her voice was laced with hatred. "How many meals did I miss, my stomach an empty pit? How many nights did I cry out? Desperate for a meal, to see Mama, to have a drink of water? How many times did my bones *ache* from your fists? My first memory is of your anger, your face bloated with rage. For what? What did I do that made you hate me so much?" She did not wait for an answer. "You deserve a death far more painful than the one you will receive, but know it comes from the bottom of my heart—there is not a *shred* of me that does not want you to die tonight."

She stepped into the circle, feeling the power of the ancient earth that gave her energy. It shuddered down her spine.

"You will have nothing to return to; your mother won't dare let you in when she discovers what you have done. Dabbling in witchcraft—she will be the first to light your pyre," Victor growled.

"She never wanted you," he added when he could not provoke a reaction from Red. "She was pleased when the opportunity to trade your life for power came up."

"*We* shall see," Red said with a smile. "But you won't."

She brought the blade to her father's throat, grabbing his hair and yanking his head back. He hissed, baring his teeth with the ferocity she had seen in him more than once. But Red's serenity remained, her face neutral and placid as a gentle lake. It was so easy to sever his flesh and arteries, his windpipe, as she dragged the blade to the right. It felt like slicing butter.

It was so easy. It was too easy.

The gagging and writhing came, and Red stepped back as his blood sprayed from the gaping wound in his neck. The Wolf released his grip on her father, and he slumped forward, choking out his last dying breaths as his blood seeped into the wood and dirt, spilling around him. The metallic scent soured the room as the light left Victor's eyes.

Red exhaled deeply, any lingering resentment leaving her body. For the first time in her life, she felt peace.

37

OCLEAU

THE YEAR OF THE CURSE

MATTHIAS

A slap woke Matthias. He jerked out of sleep to find himself face-to-face with Azalea. His unadjusted eyes observed a young child in a white nightgown standing behind her. He snapped fully awake when he realized who he was looking at—his daughter, Eliise.

A twist in his gut at the sight of her made him sit up, but his head spun—he realized that Azalea had drugged him. "W—" His words fell, his tongue numb. He tried again. "What did you do to me?"

"You needed rest after what you went through," Azalea told him. "But now there is work to do."

"Work? Why is... Why is she here?" Matthias lifted his head, but it weighed a thousand pounds.

"It is time to rid ourselves of loose ends. Ana dies tonight," Azalea informed him, thrusting a cup of water into his hands. "You must prove your sincerity to your family. You must prove to me that you do not love that woman. You have to be purified of your past in order to create a future. Don't you want that? A real future?" She didn't allow him to answer.

"My end of the bargain was that you remain here. Now we must seal that promise."

He drank with vigor, unable to contain himself. It was no wonder she was able to drug him so easily; he trusted her when she handed him something to drink. After he satisfied his thirst, he put down the cup and took a deep breath. His eyes raised to meet his daughter's. She looked back shyly, clearly uncomfortable in this strange house filled with unusual smells and new people.

"You said only he would get hurt," Matthias reminded Azalea.

"She will turn me in, Matthias, and your hands are just as filthy as mine. You had your hands deep in witchcraft this month, too. Now, to use Blaez, to make him do what we need done, you must sacrifice your child."

How does she even know about Eliise? That damned crow. Matthias's senses were coming back. He threw off his blankets. "Absolutely not."

"I will not sacrifice Juniper," Azalea said, her tone hinting at something more. "You will sacrifice the child you left behind. Remember, Matthias—you left her to grow up hungry, without parents. I know you never wanted her. Otherwise, you would have taken her with you."

"What will happen to her?" Matthias asked. "I will not have her harmed."

"We shall see. It has never been done before," Azalea replied, then she dug through the pocket of her skirt and withdrew a scroll. "I am not all evil, my son; it will be up to the Wolf what happens to your daughter."

Matthias could tell that Blaez was a good person, and he hoped that he would see Eliise and leave her be, that her presence would be enough. He hadn't wanted a child with Riina, not at first. He couldn't have taken her with him when he left. She was better off in the orphanage than on the run with him. *Things are different now.*

He glanced again at his quivering daughter, his last reminder of Riina. He had Ana now, and this time he could take Eliise.

"Where is Juniper?" Matthias asked.

A flicker of something crossed over Azalea's eyes, but her face remained impassive. She glared at him. "Juniper has gone to ensure Blaez does not try to leave; that will be his first course of action. We need him close, so we must act quickly."

"Why not send your beast of a bird?" Matthias asked.

"A crow cannot stop a man from leaving, but a witch can."

"If a hand is laid on her…"

"Matthias, enough," she snapped. "We have work to do."

Matthias stood up and let the blood rush back to all parts of his body. After a moment of recovery, his eyes moved to his child, a daughter he never wanted, a daughter that he would have to give up. Her hair was fair, closer to Riina's blonde than his dark locks. But she had the same facial features.

"Good evening, Eliise." Matthias crouched down before his daughter.

"I'm scared," she whispered.

"I know," he whispered back. "But everything will be okay. I promise."

He rose and glanced at Azalea, his eyes narrowing. "I cannot forgive you for what you are making me do."

"You could never forgive me either way, what difference does one more life make?" Azalea snapped. She handed the scroll to Matthias, holding it out to him with steady, wrinkled hands. When he reached for it, she snatched it back. "But first, we make a blood oath."

"What is a blood oath?" Matthias frowned.

"A bond that, if broken, results in death," she told him simply. "I need you to promise me you will remain with me for however long I live."

Matthias ran his hand over his face but knew he had to accept. He glanced at his daughter, he hoped that his plan would work—even if he had to remain here with his mother. Already he thought of all the ways he could kill her, but she had lived this long and had excellent survival instincts. Plotting her murder was too obvious, but he knew for certain Azalea would use Juniper as a sacrifice to kill Ana if Matthias did not use Eliise. Or else she would kill her another way. Azalea was perfectly capable of killing Ana in any way she wished; she was making Matthias do it to break him.

Matthias had to play her game for now. If he did this right, Ana would not die. The only way he could ensure Ana lived was by doing this himself.

"Very well," he replied at last.

Azalea smiled gently, then grabbed a dagger from a table. She placed the blade against her palm, her eyes flitting up to Matthias's. "Repeat after me, exactly as I say."

Azalea sliced her palm, blood spilling out the sides of her grip and onto the floor.

Eliise gasped and backed up a few steps.

Matthias quickly took hold of the dagger and did the same to his own hand, wincing at the pain of cutting where he already had been cut earlier.

"*Alligant dictum sanguine nostro,*" Azalea chanted.

Matthias repeated the words, "*Alligant dictum sanguine nostro.*"

He felt the power of the oath flow through him like the very blood he spilled was being reintroduced to his veins. He'd had enough witchcraft for his entire lifetime, but he was not done yet. When the impact wore off, and the oath was in place, he turned to his daughter.

Azalea held out the scroll, and he took it.

"What do I do?" he asked.

"Read the scroll and mean every word. Then speak Ana's last name."

Matthias looked at Eliise, the terror etched on her face, and wondered if she would ever be able to look at him again. Tears welled in her eyes, too big for her face, nearly identical to her mother's. Matthias crouched down before her and placed his hands on her tiny shoulders, he whispered, "It will be okay."

He could feel Azalea's eyes boring into him, burning a hole right through his back. Unrolling the scroll, he read it in his mind first and then took a shaky breath.

"'Hatred consumes; feed this craving once and for all, end the reasoning for my enmity. End the blood that drips from the family, end their reign. I sacrifice my living, breathing daughter; yours to take as you will. Take that which I love to end that which I hate.'" He took a deep breath, the last name gliding effortlessly from his lips. *"Tamm."*

A gust of wind forced the front door open, and an invisible force slammed into his daughter's tiny body. She lunged forward, then stopped, her body suspended in midair before she was twisted upright. Her eyes rolled back in her head, making Matthias jerk back in disgust. The shell of a girl, a puppet to the curse, turned around, her feet shuffling on the uneven floorboards, and she walked gracefully out the opened door and disappeared into the black depths of the forest.

Matthias stood up, shaken by what he had witnessed. Deeply disturbed, he could do nothing but wait to see what unraveled in the morning. *Blaez will not bear the blame tomorrow.* A smile threatened to show on his expression as he realized how to break free from the hold she had on him. *Tomorrow, she will burn, and I will taste freedom again.*

"Are you happy now, Mother?" Matthias asked sourly.

"Yes," Azalea replied. From the look in her eyes, she believed she had everything she wanted in the palm of her hands.

38

SILVANIA

THE YEAR OF THE MOON

RED

Silence filled the house in the woods.
A distant raven quorked, reminding all those inside that there was still work to do. A dull gray light filled the forest, showing the companions that the darkness of the night was done and the worst had come and gone. It was time to fulfill promises and break the Wolf's curse.

The scurry of a rat startled everyone except Sorin, who reached her hand down and let Lucien climb up her arm to perch on her shoulder. She leaned her head over and nuzzled her faithful familiar.

"Are you alright, Red?" Alina asked.

Red leaned her head back as she inhaled, filled with newfound confidence in who she was becoming. She grinned, her smile crooked and dangerous. *This power feels so good.*

"Yes," she replied as she breathed out. "I have never felt so *powerful* before."

"Careful now," the Wolf warned her. "You're starting to sound like your ancestors."

"We have work to do," Sorin said. "Get his body out of here."

Everyone looked down at Victor, lifeless and surrounded by a pool of his blood. The Wolf stepped forward, grabbing the corpse by his arms and lifting the upper half of his body. Tatiana quickly stepped up to grab his legs to keep them from dragging and messing up the circle. The sound of their shuffling followed them through the front door; shortly thereafter, a loud thump as the carcass was thrown lazily off the porch. They returned within a few moments, all eyes turning to Red.

"How do we proceed?" Red asked.

Sorin brushed her hair back, tangles stopping her blood-stained fingers from reaching the tips of her dark locks. There was a splash of blood on her cheeks; all of them were covered in the viscous liquid. The entire night had proven to be a bloodbath.

But it will all be over soon, Red thought. *We have created a new bedtime story for parents to tell their children about witches and covens.*

There was only one more piece of the puzzle before the Wolf would be set free from his curse, and Silvania would face a new kind of wrath. One that may give them the courage to rise up against their abusers. *Against cruel men like my father,* Red thought.

"You," Sorin said, pointing to the Wolf, "in the circle. On your knees."

He eyed her, untrusting, then walked with careful steps into the bloody circle. He got on his knees, a flash of memory from a very, very long time ago tickling the edges of his mind. He winced.

"Red, kneel outside the circle," Sorin commanded, glancing at the ancient scroll, looking for answers or guidance; after a moment, she accepted she was on her own. She had all the ingredients to undo the curse, she had confidence in her ability to carry it through without making mistakes. *There is no backing out,* she reminded herself, *all I can do is try.* No additional lives would be lost should they fail; Red's grandmother and father deserved their deaths.

"Alina, you need to draw the blood from Red," Sorin decided. "Red, you must give it willingly. I presume you will give it willingly to Alina, no?"

Red looked up at Alina, a flush of rouge filling her cheeks. She nodded quickly.

"*Summum hoc imperii,*" Sorin whispered. She closed her eyes, holding the scroll in her hands. She repeated the words again. "*Summum hoc imperii!*"

Alina grabbed the blade and placed it against Red's palm, where the cut she made was now a scar. Red lifted her other hand and gripped the Wolf's. With fingers interlocked, the warmth spread through their collective grasp. Red held her left hand over the circle, Alina hesitating for only a second; she did not want to harm Red but knew she had to.

Lilianna joined the chanting, followed by Tatiana. Their collective voices rang out like a choir, starting quietly as they felt the words dance over their tongues. Then they chanted as one, their voices filling the entire house. They linked hands to create a stronger power, feeling it surge through each of them as they focused on a single goal —freeing the Wolf from his torment.

Alina spoke the words, and just as the blade dug into Red's flesh, the front door flung wide.

Everyone jerked to a halt, the chanting and energy disappearing like a candle being blown. Heads turned towards the intruder, a bulky man whose frame filled the door and blocked out almost all the light. His eyes darted from the young women to the man kneeling on the floor. There was no confusion as he studied them; it was only too obvious what was going on, especially with the corpse of Red's father lying right outside the house.

"Witchcraft!" the man shouted.

The Wolf went to stand when Sorin shouted, "No! Stay there. You will break what we have started."

Alina was the only one armed, so she stepped away from Red and the circle. Red reached for her, only managing to grab her skirt, the sleek fabric sliding from her fingers with ease. Alina approached the man with the dagger high. In response, the man raised the ax he held and brought it high over his head. Blood lust took over his expression as he had no trouble killing a witch: he would be hailed as a savior if he killed Alina where she stood.

Red jumped to her feet. *I can't let her die for me.*

Screams sounded all about the room in protests and shrieks. As the ax came down, Red shoved Alina out of the way. The *thunk* of metal penetrating flesh and bone instantly silenced the shouting. Everyone stood stunned by what they witnessed, unable to believe it was real.

Red stumbled back, her hands reaching to her chest to feel the ax embedded there. She looked up at the man who killed her, blinking in disbelief. Her head lowered. She stared at the ax as she fell backward, a soft exhale escaping her lips before she slammed into the floor. He stepped forward, gripping the handle of the ax that protruded from Red's body; he was ready to kill them all, yanking on the weapon to try and rip it from Red's body. It was stuck, so he pulled again, harder.

The Wolf stood up, caring not about the witchcraft, for it would do no good now that Red was dead. Before he could launch his attack, Alina slipped in between them and plunged the dagger into the intruder's throat as he leaned down for the ax. She withdrew the blade, and blood gushed from the wound, his artery severed. The man stumbled backward, grabbing at his throat in a desperate attempt to stop the bleeding. He stumbled out the door and collapsed on the porch with a gurgle.

The dagger clattered to the floor.

39

OCLEAU

THE YEAR OF THE CURSE

AZALEA

It was a beautiful, ashen day. The gray clouds blocked the sunlight, and snow gently fell like tears for the lives lost overnight. The whole town was in mourning, though scarcely anyone knew what events occurred. As they woke for their morning tasks, begrudgingly leaving the warmth of their beds to face the chill of the winter morning, nothing seemed out of place. But already a body had been found, and the authorities had been contacted. Already they had discovered the culprit.

They did not come knocking gently; they pounded upon the door. Though Azalea opened the door to welcome them into her home, masking her shock at the intrusion, they were not gentle as they arrested her. Two large men grabbed either arm, one gripping her hair as they dragged her down the stairs. Stumbling over her feet and trying to retain her boldness and bravery in the face of peril, Azalea twisted her ankle on the stairs as they yanked her. Gritting her teeth together, she decided they would not get the satisfaction of breaking her.

She would not cry out; she would not beg. She would show them that no witch feared them, even if it were not true.

They did not bother dragging Azalea into town. It was too far, and Ocleau had not yet built a community pyre for executions as other towns had. They brought her Juniper's body; they had unearthed her from the snow that came over the course of the night and flipped her so she was on her back. Seeing the gaping wound in her throat gave Azalea no satisfaction. It had caused her great pain to desecrate Juniper's corpse, slashing and peeling back her flesh so it looked like Blaez had done it. Seeing her daughter, frozen stiff and drained of life, she felt as though she was only seeing it now for the first time.

Beside her body stood her brother.

Azalea wanted to shout at him for being a traitor, turning his back on her the moment he could. She realized the mistake she made—the blood oath would last for as long as she lived, so Matthias plotted her death.

Azalea then spotted the Wolf, Blaez, his eyes now crow black. His hands were pulled over his head, twisted behind his back so that his joints might pop, and tied to a branch above him. He hung his head low. Stark naked, and covered in blood, on his knees. Next to him was a pyre.

They released Azalea, and she fell to her knees; a large clump of her hair was ripped violently from her scalp. Blood trickled over her forehead. Her breathing increased as she willed herself not to scream in agony. Throbbing pain in her head, hands, and ankles consumed her for a moment as they paused. She was yanked to her feet and forcibly tied to the pyre.

Over the cries of *"Witch!"* Azalea heard a softer voice.

Blaez was speaking so quietly, and only Azalea was close enough to hear him.

"Just kill me," he begged. He did not seem to care that the one who had cursed him was there, he did not even seem to notice her arrival as blinded as he was by grief. He repeated the words over and over, like a chant that he was forced to speak for the rest of his days.

He had killed his wife; Azalea knew it. She could feel it in his agony rippling through the forest, as strong as the power within the earth. Yet, when she looked at her son, he looked smug. As though he knew something she did not. Her eyes narrowed into slits as she glared at him; what was he hiding?

"Blaez Kõiv, we hear your plea of guilt and place the deaths of Ana Kõiv and Juniper Luca at your hand. We also condemn you for conspiring with a witch and carrying out unspeakable acts that are forbidden in this town," the mayor spoke. "Do you have anything to say to defend yourself, or do you still claim the guilt of such?"

Azalea's mind reeled.

Kõiv. She looked up at her son, a gasp escaping her lips. *He tricked me.*

Her lip curled in disgust; she wanted to shout and scream, but it would do no good.

It was her fault for being sloppy. In her confidence that no one would dare stand up to her, she had misjudged the ruthlessness of her righteous, do-gooder son. He had proven that he had the guts to kill an innocent. *He's not so different from me, after all.*

She would not survive this day, but her son would. *How did he do it?* Azalea wondered. *How did he fool me? He truly is my own flesh and blood.*

"Just kill me," Blaez said again, this time lifting his head and showing the utter despair only a truly broken man would reveal.

"Very well."

Matthias stood with his hands at his side; his steely gaze penetrated through the crowd and burned into his mother. The discovery of Juniper horrified him—she was the only person he believed safe from Azalea.

Matthias spoke then. "This man is not guilty."

Everyone looked at him, hushed whispers about him filled the snowy air. Some people began to shout their thoughts, but Matthias held up his hand to silence them. Matthias now stood with authority he never demonstrated before, as if determined more than anything to put all of the blame upon Azalea. To expose her for the years of torment she saw as survival.

"Explain yourself." The tall man directed his attention to Matthias.

"This woman killed her daughter, my sister."

A communal gasp echoed through the crowd.

"Yes, my mother is a witch. But I have never had any part in what she has done. Many of you recall I grew up here but left some years ago. To say I regret my return is an understatement. Azalea Luca may have birthed me, but she is no mother. She has killed so many innocents; perhaps someone you loved, perhaps a neighbor. She killed Juniper. Many of you knew my sister and were helped by her; she was a kind person. She killed this man's wife. He is not to blame for either death today."

"No!" Blaez roared at last, then he began to shake, sobbing though he had nothing left in him. "I did it. I did it! Just kill me!"

He was begging for his death even though he was not to blame.

He had been shattered.

"He is right," Azalea spoke at last, knowing she would not live either way. "I killed my daughter. I killed his wife. I turned him," she jutted her head towards Blaez, "into a monster that will haunt each and every one of you—"

"Enough!" Matthias yelled. "She has admitted her guilt, this trial is concluded. Let us carry out her sentence."

The man looked at Matthias, considering his words before nodding. "Would you do the honor of burning Ocleau's first witch?"

"The honor is well received." Matthias's words were wicked. Matthias looked at Blaez first. "What will happen to him?"

Blaez looked up, his hollow black eyes pleading for a death he would not receive. He no longer begged because he no longer had the will to speak. His muscles were taut, his head hung in shame. He was not ashamed of his nakedness; he was ashamed of what he had become. Everything he had done in the last few days had been for his wife.

Azalea suspected that everything he had done since he had met her was for her benefit. He had no idea she tricked him, that she went behind his back with Matthias.

They used an innocent to appear as Ana's corpse, defaced and desecrated enough to not be able to tell the difference, she realized. Blaez was not the monster that Azalea created; her own son was.

"Exile." The man decided. Two men rushed to Blaez and cut the rope; he fell forward, hunched and devastated. Someone threw him some clothing, but he did not move. His messy hair hung in the snow, slick with sweat; his body had turned red in the freezing cold, but he made no effort to cover or warm himself. He did not look up when the man continued. "You are hereby exiled from Ocleau and surrounding towns. Your name will cross borders, and you will not find sanctuary here. Return, and your head will be ours to take. Consider this a gift; the blood on your hands is not your sin to bear."

Blaez did not move.

"The torch." Matthias reached out for the flame to light the pyre, eager.

"Matthias," Azalea said when he was standing before her with the torch in hand. She was not going to plead for her life like Blaez pled for his death. These were to be the last words to her son and to anyone; they would not be wasted. "You are no better than me."

He stared at his mother, his expression blank. He allowed her the last word, a small smirk crossing his lips. He won.

He said nothing as he lowered the torch. The dry wood caught quickly, smoke billowing in the wind before it moved towards Azalea.

Taking one final breath of fresh air, she held it as the smoke reached her. Her feet grew warmer, sweat beading on her skin. As her clothing caught fire, Azalea felt searing pain as her skin singed. Her lungs burned with every breath she took. Her only solace was to look up and hope some clean air could penetrate the thick smoke. It did not help, but she was able to open her eyes once again. Overhead, despite the heavy smoke, Aegidius sat upon a sturdy branch, overseeing his witch's death.

She finally allowed herself to scream as the fire consumed her. She had promised herself she would remain silent, but the pain was too much. Never before had she been so aware of her body and her mortality. Only a minute or two had gone by since Matthias had lit the pyre, her own son becoming the bringer of her death. She could not blame him; he played her game, and he played it better than she had. She took her final, smoke-filled breath before death crept in to claim her.

It came as a relief.

40

SILVANIA

THE YEAR OF THE MOON

BLAEZ

Red writhed as Alina dropped to her knees and let the dagger fall to the ground. The clatter of the dagger was masked by the flurry of words coming from Alina's mouth. None of it was comprehensible, but the Wolf knew what she was saying. He shouted similar things when he discovered Ana's death.

Red was mumbling, a gurgle of blood disturbing her words. But he could hear it clearly. *"Summum hoc imperii..."*

She was trying to finish breaking his curse. Something inside of him curled in on itself, his stomach twisting. Shutting his eyes, he waited for the relief that would come. But the words tapered off. He shot his eyes open and looked at the two women next to him on the floor.

Alina reached her hands around the back of Red's neck and lifted her head, but it fell back down when Alina released her.

Rose Luca was dead, and he was still cursed.

Alina's hands fluttered over the wound, unsure how to heal such a gaping wound. Her hands pressed against it, and when Red didn't flinch, Alina realized it was for naught.

"No," she whimpered. Then she looked up at the faces all staring at her. "Save her, Sorin. Someone, anyone…"

"She's gone," Sorin replied solemnly.

The Wolf inhaled deeply, looking up at the ceiling where he noticed a streak of blood from the massacre. He should have known better; that a handful of young witches in way over their heads couldn't break a curse created by an evil, seasoned witch. A deep, carnal scream that had been built for four hundred years finally came out. His yell shook the house, and when it was over, he felt no better.

His eyes went back to the family tree. It was a punch to his gut as he saw her name there.

Ana's name.

How this eluded him all these years, he did not know. How could he have been so easily played not just by Azalea but by Matthias and Ana as well? After everything he did for her, she had the decency to curse him like this for eternity, to make him think he had her blood on his hands for four hundred years—it surprised him, but it all added up.

She never wanted to be with me. Yet to get rid of him in such a brutal manner, that's what would have broken him if he hadn't already been shattered hundreds of times.

She had children with him. With Matthias Luca.

He gritted his teeth, leaving the circle and flopping down on the couch behind him in defeat. In life, no one came out unscathed. Possibly the last Luca was dead on the floor, and he should have been thankful. Yet he felt guilty for her death. The curse still remained, the scroll perfectly intact in Sorin's shaking hands. He would be used again and again. When he woke to the woman he thought was Ana, torn apart, he wanted to die. After all he had done, it had been so she would be safe. Knowing now that she betrayed him, used his softness, and abused his kindness… It made everything so much worse.

Why hadn't she just let him leave?

"What happened?" Tatiana asked.

"The protection spell didn't work," Lilianna said.

"She was protected from the Wolf, not this man," Sorin said in defense of her spell.

"What about Alina? How is she protected from love?" Tatiana shouted. "I do not understand!"

"I do," Alina said with a stony look on her face. "The only way to be protected from love is to have nothing to love."

"She is right," the Wolf said, glancing her way and offering a look that he hoped conveyed sympathy. Alina didn't respond, her marble expression impenetrable. It would remain that way for the rest of her life, he knew; he wore the same face after he thought he murdered Ana.

The memory flashed before him.

Blaez woke up in the snow just outside his home. He was nearly frozen, there was no warmth left in him as he tuned into his surroundings. Scrambling to his feet, he noticed the blood, splatters of it all around him, over the outer walls of the house, a trail leading to the side. He knew it before he saw it, and yet he couldn't stop himself from walking towards the carnage; he drew the blood, he took the life, the least he could do was face it.

Blaez's stomach protested. He retched over the snow when he saw it, the woman he loved desecrated, parts of her intact, others a distance away. Her chest was opened up, organs and entrails spilling from her torso. One arm was raised above her head, frozen solid in the snow, fingertips black and purple where they weren't covered in blood. The other arm was a few meters away, detached at the elbow, with crystalized blood in the snow. Her shin was snapped in the center, the bone jutting out. There was nothing left of her face, just shreds of skin and bone, teeth scattered about like gruesome seeds.

But he knew it was Ana.

"What do we do now?" Lilianna asked, snapping Blaez out of his daze.

He looked up, seeing all four women looking at him. Alina remained on her knees, clutching Red's cooling hand, silently sobbing. Sorin held the crumpled scroll in her hand while Lilianna and Tatiana held onto one another.

I owe them nothing; all they brought was more death, more blood on my hands, Blaez thought. *These girls are no different than any of the sacrifices I've had cross my path before.*

Although he would never trust a witch, these four were not Azalea Luca.

"I can keep you safe for a time," he said. "I can help you relocate somewhere else."

"Why would you help us? We failed at freeing you from the curse," Sorin asked.

He looked at Red. "She died trying to help me. Trying to change. She fought the darkness inside her, the darkness that was in her blood…I owe it to her to help you."

"No," Alina growled. "We finish this."

All eyes turned to her, but the Wolf refused to accept that it could be done. Too many lives were lost because of him; he claimed Red's death as his fault. One more name added to the ledger, somehow the most painful one of all. All she sought in life was to be free of her abusers, something he understood to his core.

Alina wiped a stream of tears from her eyes, smearing Red's blood over her. "Red might…"

He knew she was trying to say the words, but she couldn't admit she was dead.

"*Be gone,*" Alina choked, "but she did it to protect us. Maybe…"

"She needs to be the one," Sorin whispered softly to Alina.

"We have to try! It's what she would have wanted!" Alina shouted back, shaking violently now.

Tatiana spoke then, brushing her tangles behind her ear. "Alina, you initiated Red. We thought perhaps that interfered with the protection spell. Maybe your connection to Red is stronger than we think. Oh, Sorin, do you think it is possible?"

Sorin glanced around, eyes landing on the Wolf. "Let us give this one more try."

He inhaled deeply, then rose from his spot on the couch. Every bone in his body ached as though four hundred years were finally catching up to him. Without being told, he knelt back in the circle. He noted a trickle of blood from Red's corpse slithering towards him. Caught off guard by Alina crawling towards him, he was startled when she grabbed his hand and pulled it towards her. She flashed her palm to him, showing a scar across her palm.

The women around them began to chant again, repeating Red's last words, picking up where she left off. *"Summum hoc imperii."*

It was Tatiana who held the blade this time.

Alina took the Wolf's hand and asked, "What is your name?"

A feeling of peace sunk into his weary bones as he remembered. "Blaez."

"Summum hoc imperii." Lilianna, Sorin, Alina, and Tatiana chanted together, as though they were one.

"Invoco terrae, luna, sanguine. Liber Blaez," Tatianna said the words as she sliced Alina's palm; her blood, bound with Rose Luca's, dribbled to the floor. Three generations of Luca blood surrounded him.

He watched with fascination and horror as it touched him, soaking through his trousers. The ache in his chest, carried with him for so many years, tightened. Keeling over, he gasped. This pain he remembered from four hundred years before forced him to throw his head back, his spine bending as though he was shifting into a wolf one final time. Smoke as black as night emerged from his mouth, the curse pouring out of him.

For a moment, he felt nothing at all; he was suspended from reality.

He managed to breathe out, "Thank you."

And as the curse disappeared, so did his life.

~

Lilianna spoke first. Her petite frame knelt beside the man, a hand on his shoulder as though she were comforting him. "He had green eyes."

Sorin looked at Alina; there was something different about her. Something broken.

"We must bury her," Sorin announced. "Then we take back the town."

They vacated the house of death as a raven observed them overhead. Alina and Sorin carried Red's body out into the forest, where they agreed she should be buried. They took turns hauling dirt with a single shovel, the four of them splitting the workload. Alina only relinquished the spade when Sorin forced the shovel out of her blistered and bloody hands. Sorin knew the labor distracted her from the pain of losing Red.

They lowered her body into the grave, and Sorin placed the now wordless scroll in with her. All four of them began to push the dirt over her with their hands. Witches achieved their most basic power from the Earth, their flesh absorbing that power as they buried one of their own. As they finished, they paused to wipe their tears away with soiled hands. Alina sank to the ground and wept, comforted by the hushed, soothing whispers of the sisters.

Only Sorin did not cry.

When it was done, and Rose Luca's body returned to the Earth, it felt like waking from a nightmare. One they would slowly recover from. In time each of them would heal, the wounds slowly closing.

EPILOGUE
SILVANIA

A na held her belly, the life growing within her shifting and pressing hard against her organs. She watched from below as Matthias finished patching the roof. The home they purchased had ample land, but the building was falling apart at the seams. Even from below, she could see Matthias knitting his brow, his face pinched as he concentrated.

He'd borne a disdainful expression since that night in Ocleau. The night he paid the orphanage matron Kaisa Tamm to come to her house. Ana remembered it well.

Blaez returned home with the cure for Ana, but Matthias had given it to her earlier that day. Everyone was there at once—Blaez arrived to give the cure to Ana, but before he could enter, his body betrayed him, forcing him to shift into the Wolf. Then the child arrived, possessed.

She watched him, black as night, with eyes that would have made any normal person shriek in terror. His eyes had locked onto the child, and Ana clutched her niece tightly; the Wolf approached. The beast smelled the child, who whimpered and cried in terror. Then he shuddered and turned away; simply seeing the child was enough. The sacrifice had been made, and the Wolf's decision was to allow the child to live. Blaez's good-hearted nature came through even as a beast; this was the only mercy Azalea granted him.

When Ana was able to move, when the frozen terror released its hold on her, she slipped out the moment Eliise was safe, wrapping her in something warm and whisking her through the back door, leaving the confused Kaisa Tamm alone with the beast.

Ana was already far away, but she made sure to cover Eliise's ears when the screaming began. They scurried into the woods, where Matthias would meet them the next night so they could begin their journey to find a better life. All Ana packed were the herbs to help her become pregnant, a change of clothes for her and Eliise, and some food—though not enough that anyone who looked through the house would know.

Ana watched Matthias change the night he met them after he had his mother executed. After finding his sister dead, her body ice cold in the snow. He would never be the same, but Ana reminded herself that she never really knew Matthias—Riina did. Ana still envied her dead sister for being able to love Matthias before he changed, and sometimes she pretended to be Riina for him. She tried to be the version of Riina that she remembered.

On those days, Matthias loved her.

Some days Matthias couldn't even look at her, hatred brewing between them. He blamed her for this, and she blamed him for that; even Eliise couldn't escape the unexplainable resentment that bloomed, insidious and spreading like a disease. Eliise grew jealous of the baby growing in Ana's womb, fearing that she would not be loved. Fearing that she would be replaced.

When they found the scroll with the curse upon it, they wondered how it got there. It followed them to their brand-new home. They knew the Wolf had, too; Blaez lurked in the Mørke Forest, waiting to be called upon. He would forever be tied to the Lucas, to the curse, just as they would.

Ana watched as Matthias stepped down from the roof onto the ladder, and part of her hoped it would topple, taking him with it.

ACKNOWLEDGMENTS

The list of people I need to thank is endless.

My parents, for supporting me in every chaotic decision I've made, eventually leading me to decide that being an author was the only path for me.

My friends and peers who helped me carve out a place for myself in the writing community, both online and in person.

A special thank you to Kate P., the biggest cheerleader in my life, who has been there for me every step of the way.

Kate S., Katie Y., Larissa C., thank you all for being the originals who helped shape this book.

And thank you to Cassandra, Tiff, and everyone else at Quill & Crow for taking a chance not only on my book, but my series that I hold so near and dear to my heart. The Blood Bound Series finally has a real home.

ABOUT THE AUTHOR

Sabrina Voerman is a West Coaster with a penchant for visiting the numerous cemeteries across Vancouver Island. With a profound love of fairy tales and all things witchy, she draws her inspiration from the nature around her, allowing it to bleed into her storytelling. She is always seeking new adventures and places to explore, either in life or in her writing. When she isn't traversing all Vancouver Island has to offer, she can be found with a cup of coffee either reading a book or writing one.

COMING SOON FROM SABRINA VOERMAN

Ashen Heart: The Blood Bound Series Book Two (Spring 2024)

Song of the Sea: The Blood Bound Series Book Three (Autumn 2024)

Blood Queen: The Blood Bound Series Book Four (Autumn 2025)

THANK YOU FOR READING

Thank you for reading *Blood Coven*. We deeply appreciate our readers, and are grateful for everyone who takes the time to leave us a review. If you're interested, please visit our website to find review links. Your reviews help small presses and indie authors thrive, and we appreciate your support.

Other Titles by Quill & Crow

The Ancient Ones Trilogy

The Quiet Stillness of Empty Houses

Her Dark Enchantments

TRIGGER INDEX

- Child abuse
- Domestic abuse
- Gaslighting/Manipulation
- Murder/Violence
- Sexual assault/incest (implied/off-screen)

Printed in Great Britain
by Amazon